FISHING WITH LIZA

Ryan S. Pack

Ryan S. Pack

© 2014

Ryan S. Pack

ISBN-13: 978-0-9860564-7-5

Second Edition

This book is dedicated to my sister Rebecca for showing me how strong children can be, and to my own children, for continuing to prove it every day. I would also like to dedicate this to parents everywhere. There can be no greater joy nor terror than that a parent feels when their child looks into their eyes and expects them to make it all better. Anyone can be a genetic donor, it takes a special soul to be a parent. And to those of you whose chosen profession is the saving of lives, civilian or military, know that you fight the good fight, and you do it well. The thanks you deserve can never be adequately expressed.

<u>Chapter One</u>

"Control, SH-3, Do you copy, over?"

The under-dash mike squawked; the tinny voice of Tiffany Brown amplified throughout the truck. In the passenger seat, Byron Williamson cringed down even farther in the seat, as if he wished it would eat him up.

"SH-3, acknowledge, I know you can hear me."

Byron winced, squeezing his eyes into painful little slits, and pressed his fists to his temples.

"Uh, Ram, you think that we, maybe, ought to answer her?" asked Jack Blaire, Byron's partner this hateful Tuesday night. He kept snatching furtive glances over at Byron, sweat shining through his buzz-cut despite the unit's air-conditioning. Byron opened his eyes, a faded-out species of blue that had once been one of his more attractive features. Now, they were blood-shot and weary, and never seemed to focus on any one thing for more than a moment or two. He turned his head slowly, as if the pivoting action was accompanied by the sound of rusty hinges opening. He fixed his baleful stare on Jack, and watched him squirm about nervously.

"You want to answer her? Answer her", he said dismissively, his voice dead and hollow, "Just play 'I'll Think of Something' again".

"Jesus, Ram. Any chance we could listen to the radio for a while? I mean, I like Mark Chestnut as much as anyone, but that's all we've listened to for the last three hours. Too much of a good thing, you know?"

Byron smiled in that empty way he had, the grin never seeming to reach his eyes. He looked over at Jack, who suddenly found the road very interesting, and made a great show of checking his rearview mirror before changing lanes.

"How about you play my music and answer Control before I twist your fucking head off? How about *that*?"

"Sure, Ram, no sweat, man. I was just wondering."

"That will only lead to a whole new world of hurt, Jack. Leave the wondering to your elders."

Byron fell back into the hard vinyl seat, blowing out a long breath. He wasn't mad at Blaire; he knew that, it was just that the little bastard was the closest person to him at the moment. He considered apologizing to him, and then decided it was too much of a hassle. Everything was too much of a hassle. Work was nothing but an unending pain in his ass, punctuated by an occasional bout of stupidity. He closed his eyes and reached for his army-issue canteen. He rolled off the top and took a long drink. Orange liquid gurgled down his throat. His Adam's apple worked, and he sighed. The smell of Popov vodka and Sunny Delight filled the cab of the ambulance.

Jack looked over at Byron, wanting to say something about drinking on duty, and then decided against it. Ram wasn't kidding, he knew. If Jack said anything else out of line tonight, Byron might very well twist his head off. He knew that Ram had been in the army, had served in Iraq, and had actually seen *war*. There might be someone to read Byron the riot act about drinking while on duty, but be *damned* if it was going to be Rebekah Blaire's boy Jack.

Byron had gone back to staring listlessly out the passenger window, watching the streetlights flicker by. He wished he was at home, *his* home, with his wife making dinner, the kids playing at his feet. Fat fucking chance of that. His wife was now making dinner in what used to be his house, his kids playing in the living room, at least if Liza was feeling up to it. His wife...well, she couldn't really be called that, not anymore. *She* sure as hell didn't answer to "wife" anymore. Samantha Williamson had gone back to Samantha Murphy almost six months ago, dropping Byron's last name like a used condom. No, there weren't going to be any more dinners at the ranch house on Beldon Street for Byron Williamson. A single, angry tear tore itself free from Byron's tightly closed eyelid, and rolled halfway down his face before he knuckled it away savagely. He sat, numb in his pain, wondering why his life had gone so tits-up, why he couldn't seem to stop drinking, why everything he saw seemed to be painted in shades of gray, wondering where the hell his army canteen had gotten to.

Six months earlier, Byron Williamson had been a man to envy. He was, in fact, envied by a great deal of his co-workers at Sacred Heart Regional Hospital, where he had been a paramedic for the last seven years. At twenty-nine years old, he was tall, handsome in an almost off-hand manner, and a remarkably happy person. He was married to his high-school sweetheart, to whom he had proposed right after graduation, before he shipped out for Basic Training in the Army. He had thought it horribly cliché, like something right out of a black-and-white movie, the soldier proposing his undying love and popping the question just before shipping out, but Samantha Murphy had been overjoyed. Christ, all they had needed was a sappy love song to score the scene.

The same could not be said for Samantha's father. Philip Murphy was an overbearing man that walked the earth with a giant chip on *both* shoulders. When Byron had asked Philip for permission to marry Samantha, his first question was "Have you knocked my daughter up, you silly shit?" Byron had been taken aback by the anger directed at him. Philip Murphy had always treated Byron with genial contempt at best up to this point, but the raw anger aimed at him now threw him. He stuttered for a moment before managing to blurt out "No, she's not *pregnant*! Why would you think *that*?"

Murphy had given Byron a scathing look. "You think I'm stupid, boy? You show up here with your hat in your hand asking to marry my daughter, but I heard you joined the Army. Why did you do that, if you're so all-fired ready to marry my little girl?"

Byron held his temper in check with an effort. "Mr. Murphy, I joined the Army so I could serve my country. There's a war on, you know. When I get out, I am going to go to college on the G.I. Bill, so I can provide a good life for Samantha."

"And if you get killed while you're over there 'serving your country'?"

Byron was getting pissed, quickly. The snide way Murphy had said "serving your country" had gotten under his skin more than anything else the man had said to him. He ground his teeth together and stood up stiffly. He looked Murphy straight in the eyes and said, "If I get killed 'serving my country', Mr. Murphy, I suppose the whole question is moot. I think Samantha would have a hard time getting a marriage license for a dead man, don't you? Now, do I have your permission, or not?"

The rest of the conversation hadn't gone much better. Had it not been for Samantha's mother, Annie, breaking into sobs, the two men might have come to blows. Byron thanked God that Samantha had been out with her friends when the conversation had taken place. He managed to leave the Murphy home without punching the sanctimonious bastard's face in, but it was a very close thing.

After a two year stint in the army as a combat medic in Iraq, he had returned to his home town of Dawkin's Mill, a little town twenty miles south of Memphis, Tennessee, and gotten a job at Sacred Heart

Hospital as a Paramedic. The hours were long, but with the overtime he was making, Byron was able to afford to start his family.

With much bad grace, Philip Murphy had given Samantha away at the wedding, but he still looked at his son-in-law like something that needed to be scraped off of the bottom of his shoe. Byron and Samantha had bought a dilapidated single-wide trailer, and moved it onto his parent's property. Byron's parents were thrilled to have their son and new daughter-in-law so close to them. Byron's mother Patricia spent much of each day either at Byron's trailer or Samantha would walk over to his parent's house. Patricia and Samantha got along very well, and grew close. Byron's father, Bill, was a retired mechanic that spent much of his time in his garage that he had converted into a workshop. Byron loved the smell of the workshop, and spent much of his free time with his father; tinkering with whatever projects his dad was working on at the moment. Byron had always been very close to his parents, and their acceptance and love of Samantha filled him with gratitude.

Patricia and Bill tried to maintain a cordial relationship with Samantha's parents, and were moderately successful in doing so, at least as far as Annie was concerned. Philip Murphy was, according to Bill Williamson, "ten pounds of shit in a five pound bag". Byron was intensely grateful Samantha hadn't been within hearing distance when Bill Williamson had espoused that particular opinion. The two families had remained polite, but distant, throughout Byron and Samantha's marriage.

They stayed in the trailer a year, and by the time Byron had saved enough money for a down-payment on the ranch house on Beldon Street, Samantha was nine months pregnant with their first child.

In an odd twist of fate, it was Byron that had been dispatched on the 911 call to transport his wife to the hospital. No one at Control had remembered Byron's new address, and had sent him without thought. Byron himself was a third of the way finished with his run sheet before he glanced up at the address again. It had struck him familiar, but he cast the thought aside. He went to so many houses in his job, and so often returned to them; sometimes they got stuck in his head. He glanced at the address once more. With a startled little grunt, he stared at his partner that day, Barry Adams, and said, "Holy shit, that's *my* house!" The seven minute ride to his house seemed to last several days.

Byron very nearly delivered his son, who they named Robert, in the back of an ambulance en route to Sacred Heart. The baby was born without a hitch, although Byron almost broke his ankle when he slipped on a broken bag of Lactated Ringer's in the E.R. He spent the remainder of that day limping around the hospital with a large, dopey grin on his face, handing out cigars.

Samantha recovered nicely, and they were all back home in two days. Byron had converted the front den of his house into a nursery, and would sometimes spend an hour at a time staring at his sleeping son. The three of them lived very well at Beldon Street, vacationing at Disney World when Robert was four. Samantha was pregnant with their second child that summer, and Byron and Robert were in the doghouse for a week when they laughed helplessly when Samantha, overcome with the Florida sun and seven months pregnant, vomited all over Goofy, much to the consternation of the gathered crowd of children.

They were living the American Dream, and Byron was very aware of his blessings. The three of them would spend summer afternoons at the lake, Byron taking them to his favorite fishing hole and teaching Robbie how to bait his hook and cast his rod. Samantha would have nothing to do with any of that process, but she loved to see Robbie's face light up when his rod tip began jerking, the promise of a monster catfish just on the other end. That he only caught small bluegill was of little consequence to either of his parents. Each fish was proudly hoisted to the bank, and the family albums were filled with pictures a tiny Robbie holding aloft a stringer full of fish.

Life was near perfect for Byron, and on Wednesday March 23, 2008. At 3:54 A.M., Samantha gave to a little girl, perfectly formed, with a thick shock of black hair. They named the baby Elizabeth, after Samantha's grandmother. Their family now seemed to be complete in a way that they hadn't even been aware it had been lacking before. Robert, far from being jealous of the new addition to the family, hovered over Liza's crib for sometimes an hour at a time, silently watching her every tiny intake of breath, not knowing he was copying his father's actions with *him*, only years before;

Byron felt extremely sorry for the boys that would come courting his little girl in the future. From all evidence, a boy getting past Robert and taking Liza had a much better chance of waltzing across water than getting his baby sister out the door. Byron couldn't suppress a grin to think that the hormone-overloaded young men that would hesitantly approach the door to their home, fearing meeting Liza's large father would instead be intercepted and intimidated by her brother before they managed to hit the doorbell. He reminded himself to make sure all the sharp instruments in the house were accounted for before any boys Liza might go out on a date with arrived to pick her up.

Liza was the picture of health, and the family was happy to the point that they sometimes got the impression that their friends were a bit sickened by the glowing sense of love and well-being that seemed to emanate from their very pores. Looking back, Byron could see the specter of the blackness that came to encompass their family so clearly, sitting quietly in the corner of the living room, a mocking smile playing across its features as the unsuspecting family basked in all that was good in the world. Sometimes, in his darker moods, or if he had been drinking more heavily than usual, Byron could see that embodiment of despair as clearly as he could see his own ever-degenerating face in the mirror when he shaved. Byron hated that figure. If he could find some way to wrap his fingers around that hateful throat, no force on earth could stop him from throttling it into non-existence, *negating* it.

Everything appeared fine, until routine blood work during a well-baby checkup after Liza's first birthday revealed a problem. Byron and Samantha sat in shock when the pediatrician grimly gave them the news: leukemia.

Thus began a nightmarish carnival ride of spinal taps, radiation, and chemotherapy. The sound of screaming children was nothing new to Byron, but it seemed to him he had never heard it with such crystalline clarity as he did when Liza, her tiny face blood-red with effort, screamed. He could not believe that her small lungs were capable of such volume. Byron attended these torturous visits, Samantha only coming out of the house when deeply medicated, and even then sometimes making it only as far as the car door before bolting back into the house.

Byron tried to explain to Robbie what was wrong with Liza, but the only thing that he could really get across was that Liza was sick. Byron had broken down and wept when Robbie had suggested that if they gave Liza *two* Flintstones vitamins a day instead of one, she might get better. Robbie, never having seen his daddy cry, broke into braying sobs of his own, and the two of them sat in the floor of Robbie's room for hours, rocking back and forth and trying so hard to draw some solace from each other, some spark of the old warmth that they had assumed they would have had forever.

Byron and Samantha became strangers to one another over the next three years, sometime visitors sharing a home. Samantha's father didn't help matters when he arrived at their home one evening quite drunk and accused Byron of ruining his daughter's life and fathering defective babies. That straw didn't break the camel's back, it *shattered* it. Philip staggered away from the Williamson home ten minutes later with one eye blackened and swollen and blood streaming from both nostrils, vomiting thin, ropy lines of blood-flecked bile. Byron was ashamed at what he had done to the man, but he had been pushed as far as he was able to go.

Byron wasn't sure when Sam began to hate him. The fist fight with her father hadn't helped matters any, he was sure. But even Samantha had been forced to agree that her father had been way over the line that night. Philip had even called several days later and given as close to an apology as Byron figured he was ever going to get. "I was drunk" wasn't one of the best explanations Byron had ever heard, but then again, it wasn't the worst either.

One morning, far into Liza's hellish treatments, Byron woke to find Samantha standing over him, her eyes glassy with hate, boring into him from across the bed they had not shared for nearly three years. His sat up on his elbows, not yet fully awake.

"What is it, Sammy?" he asked groggily, "Is it Liza all right?"

She tensed, like an animal, and for one terrifying moment, Byron thought she was going to physically attack him.

"You", she hissed, "*You*".

She threw a photo album across the room. It struck him in the chest with a dull *thump*, and flopped into his lap. Samantha whipped around and crashed out of the room. Byron heard her blundering through the house, knocking things off the wall. He remained propped up on his elbows, staring stupidly into space. Slowly, as if his arms were moving through water, he reached up into his lap and picked up the photo album. Flipping through it, not really seeing it, he wondered if he was still asleep. A picture fell out. Byron picked it up, turning it around so he could see it. It was a black and white photo of his mother's sister Amanda. There were stains on it, as if someone had sprinkled water on its surface. He sat there for several moments, unable to shake the feeling of being in a dream. Suddenly, a thought surfaced; a thought so terrible that it caused him to double over with a sudden stomach cramp.

"Oh, no", he wept, "No, Sammy, oh God, no".

He had never met his aunt Amanda. She had died when his mother was very young. She had died of leukemia.

<u>Chapter Two</u>

"SH-3, Control, do you have traffic?"

Byron jerked out of his reverie to find Blaire talking in his earnest way on the radio. When Jack spoke into the microphone, he always looked like he was talking about things of massive importance. Didn't matter if he was getting directions to a shooting victim or telling Control they were out of the unit for lunch. In the movie that constantly played in Jack Blaire's mind, he was the hero, always cool and collected in the face of disaster. Once, that had amused Byron, but now he wished the stupid son of a bitch would just shut up.

"Control, SH-3, we have a run for you. Male Caucasian, approximately forty to sixty years of age, unresponsive. Some teen-agers found him under the bridge on Martin."

"Control, do you have any further description on the patient?"

"10-4, SH-3, be advised the kids stated that the patient appears to be homeless, and very, and I quote here, 'smelly'. Stated that he was wearing a large army field jacket, and had a red, white, and blue bandanna on, over."

Byron groaned.

"Oh, fuck, no, not *him*. Jack, for the love of Christ, tell them the unit's down, tell them I'm too sick to go, tell them I ran off on you, that I died, anything."

"What is it?" Blaire asked. "Who is it? Do I know him?"

"It's that fucking Schwacter, Dennis Schwacter. You know him. Vet, Vietnam. Last took a bath 'bout the same time Reagan got popped. He stays fucked up under that bridge. We'll get there just in time to have that son of a bitch throw up on us, and then throw shit at us until we leave."

Jack thought about it for a minute, and then thumbed the mike.

"SC-3, Control. Be advised my partner is feeling very under the weather, says he may need to take a trip to E.R., over."

"Negative, SH-3, negative. Tell Williamson to take another drink and get down to that bridge, over."

Jack looked over at Byron questioningly.

"Ram?"

Byron stared angrily at his feet.

"Ram, what do you want me tell them, man?'

Byron stared angrily at his hands.

"Uh, Ram?"

Byron stared angrily at his partner.

"Fuck it. Tell them we're in route. Then tell them that after that, I'm clocking out. Going home. Getting drunk. Jacking off and going to bed."

"We copy that direct, SC-3. Be advised, we're not overly concerned with your after-hour habits, although I think there may be a nurse in Triage that could help you with at least *part* of that."

Blaire looked down at the microphone, horrified.

"Oh, shit, Ram, I swear to God I didn't mean to have it keyed up. Oh, Jesus H. Woodchuck Christ."

Byron sat, shaking his head. After a minute, he began to laugh.

"Turn on the lights and let's get this shit over with."

They turned off Martin Street onto a dirt path that led down to the bridge. Byron got out and grabbed his jump kit. He didn't bother with gloves, knowing he was most likely going to end up with whatever Schwacter had last eaten all over him. Blaire came around the back of the unit, opening the doors and reaching for the cot.

"Leave it", said Byron, "He's gonna refuse transport."

Jack hesitated, and then closed the doors back. They walked down the path, going slowly because of the mud brought on by rain earlier in the week. Flickering light filtered through the trees near the bridge. As they came around the corner of the bridge support, the smell hit them like a muted slap.

"Jeez, Ram, what the hell is that?"

Byron didn't answer. Mud squelched up around his boots, covered the bottom hem of his B.D.U. pants. A small fire was slowly burning itself out near the river's edge. Of the teens there was no sign. A snoring grunt brought Byron's attention up the bank. Lying spread-eagled on the ground was an unconscious man. Byron walked closer. Sure enough, it was Schwacter. *Damn it all*, Byron thought, *I hate this stinking shit.*

"Hey, Dennis, wake the fuck up", Byron boomed.

Schwacter remained supine on the ground.

"C'mon, you smelly bastard, get up so I can go home."

Byron walked a little closer. With rising alarm, he noticed that Schwacter didn't appear to be breathing very well.

"Hey, Schwacter, get up."

Schwacter didn't answer.

Byron knelt down over the man, his face screwed up in a grimace of disgust. Reaching down, he took the man's wrist. A pulse was there, but it was thready and very weak. Schwacter was breathing about four times a minute.

"Shit", he muttered. Turning to Blaire, he called out.

"Bring the cot and the monitor, we're gonna have to lug this piece of shit in."

Blaire turned and ran up the hill, visions of glory running through his head. Byron shook his head and turned back to Schwacter. To his surprise, the man's eyes were open. He blinked owlishly.

"Hey, Schwacter, welcome back to the land of the living."

Schwacter tried to focus on Byron. He opened his mouth to speak, and a noxious mixture of tomato soup and Mad Dog 20/20 wafted out.

"Gah", he croaked, "Guh-guh uhn."

"That's right, me foine boyo, 'gah guh-gug uhn'. Couldn't have said it better myself. A fine commentary on the human condition."

Byron began to unroll I.V. tubing. Blaire returned with the cot and the EKG monitor, and began placing leads on Schwacter's chest. He turned on the monitor, watching the spiky read-out.

They began the process of loading Schwacter onto the cot and rolling him up the hill to the ambulance. The mud made it feel like they were lugging a boulder up the embankment. Once inside, Byron sat down in the jump seat to finish his run sheet. Blaire pulled back out onto the road and turned on the lights.

"About ten minutes out, Ram. You want me to call in report?"

"Yeah, call it in. Fifty-five year-old male, history of CHF, IDDM, and hypertension. *Very* ETOH."

From these abbreviations, the hospital would be able to understand the patient's past medical history, and was intoxicated.

Jack turned to give the E.R. report, and Byron returned to his run sheet. He occasionally glanced over at the EKG. Yep, Schwacter was a sick puppy, but he would keep until they got to Sacred Heart. He finished up his run sheet, and leaned back into the seat. He had almost dozed off from the gentle rocking of the ambulance when a hoarse voice brought him back.

"Where are you taking me?" Schwacter asked, his voice weak and raspy. "Are we going to Dawkins Methodist Hospital?"

"Nope, we're heading for Sacred, pal. Closest facility."

Schwacter grimaced.

"I don't wanna go to that fucking slaughter house. You never walk outta that place. Take me to Dawkins."

Byron felt his patience, already a rare commodity, slipping.

"Listen up, Schwacter, and please listen good. You are sick. You are also a waste of space, as far as I'm concerned, but it's my job to keep you alive until we get to the hospital. I am prepared to do that. However, I am not prepared to listen to a lot of hokey bullshit about your likes and dislikes about the medical field. We are not in a taxi. We are in an ambulance. And we are going to follow the regulations set out by the great state of Tennessee, and those regulations state clearly that in the event of a life-threatening condition, we are to take you to the nearest facility. And that, my odorous friend, is exactly what we're going to do."

Schwacter craned his head around to look at Byron. He stared blearily at him with one eye.

"I know you. You're that fucking Williamson. You ain't no better'n me. You're a fucking drunk, same as me. Big war hero, right? I heard 'em talking there in E.R. Talking about how *hard* it must have been on you over there in Iraq. How *rough* you must have had it. How it must have been so *traumatic* for you. Shit."

Byron felt his hand tightening on the clip board.

"*Iraq!*" Schwacter made it sound like a curse word. "Iraq! That wasn't no war, you dipshit. I was in Vietnam, in the Green Machine. *That* was a fucking war. What'd you do over in Iraq? Medic? Huh? Fucking nose-wiper, that's what you were. Take care of little Muslim kiddies? Huh? Lemme tell ya, I *killed* little gook kids, that's what I did. They'd come up with their baskets full of grenades, and I'd pop 'em. Ungrateful bastards ran me outta the Corps over it, the fuckers. So don't take that holier-than-thou attitude with me, you prick. You ain't had no hard life. You ain't seen shit. Now, take me to Dawkins."

Byron slowly got up and came around the cot. His hands were shaking. With one large fist he reached down and grabbed Schwacter's field jacket. He pulled the man up from the cot until their noses were almost touching.

"You listen to me, you nasty *fuck*. I'll kill you. What the fuck do you know about Iraq? *Nose-wiper?* I saw kids running around on fire. I saw entire families massacred in the sand, for no good goddamned reason at all. I saw things you wouldn't understand, because you don't have the necessary equipment to get it. You need a soul for that. I've got a four year-old daughter with leukemia. I've got an ex-wife that blames me for it. And I haven't *seen* shit? I've seen more than I ever wanted to, or needed to, so shut your damned mouth."

Schwacter's face broke with a slimy grin.

"Ah, ain't that too bad? Wifey won't give you no pussy 'cause your baby girl's got sick, huh? Well, that sure does bite the old banana. Don't worry about it, though. I'll just bet that after that little girl's in the ground a few months, you'll get laid again. Women got no real sense of loyalty. She'll come around, wanting a little. You'll do all right."

Byron released Schwacter's jacket and held his hand out like it was covered in slime, which was a distinct possibility. He sat back against the bench seat, taking deep breaths and trying to calm down. After a few minutes, he felt a little more in control.

"You 'bout ready to cart me over to Dawkins now, or do you wanna have another go-round?" Schwacter asked.

Byron was about to tell Schwacter to perform fellatio on himself when the man began to buck against the straps of the cot, making a gurgling noise. Byron reflexively reached across him to grab the intubation equipment, and then stopped. He looked down into Schwacter's eyes. The man was turning an alarming shade of red, the veins around his temple bulging grotesquely. Schwacter stared up at Byron, panic livid in his eyes. Byron stared back. He bent over until he was level with Schwacter's head. When he spoke, a small puff of breath blew the greasy hair away from Schwacter's wax-clotted ear.

"Make fun of my little girl, right? Real funny, huh?" he whispered.

"Hey, Ram", Blaire yelled from the front, "You okay? Need any help?"

"No, I'm fine", he replied calmly, his eyes never leaving Schwacter's panicked face, "How far out are we?"

"About two minutes."

"Fine. Radio ahead and tell them we're bringing in a full code."

"Roger that, Cap'n!" It was impossible for Blaire to keep the joy out of his voice. This was what the job was all *about*!

Byron began to break out the intubation equipment. On the cot, Schwacter had subsided into a series of weak jerks. His eyes had rolled back into his head. His chest heaved, once, twice, thrice.

And then he was still.

Byron took the paddles off the Lifepack and placed them on Schwacter's chest. "Clear" he said, and touched off the electricity that earlier might have been useful. He grabbed Schwacter's wrist. Nothing. Taking his stethoscope, he listened to Schwacter's chest. Nothing.

Byron began to intubate Schwacter, thinking how easy it was to do when the patient wasn't flopping around. As they turned into Sacred Heart, Byron had just finished placing the tube. Jack bounded out of the unit and came around the back. They rolled Schwacter into the Emergency Room, where several nurses and a doctor stood waiting. Byron then went to get his run sheet signed, and Blaire went into the EMS room for a cup of coffee. As he stood drinking it, his gaze kept returning to where Byron Williamson stood at the nurse's desk. He didn't think anyone else had seen it; it had been gone before Ram had jumped out of the back of the unit. Blaire had seen it, though. Surely he was just tired, he thought. Surely Ram hadn't been sitting in the jump seat with a contented smile on his face?

Blaire looked off into the night. His coffee made smoke rings that wafted before his eyes. His face remained troubled.

Chapter Three

Byron woke up at 6:48 P.M., giving him exactly twelve minutes to be at Sacred Heart. *Fuck it*, he thought disjointedly, *let 'em fire me*. Not much chance of that, he supposed. He could keep his job at Sacred for as long as he wanted it, or at least as long as Doctor Donald Rutherford remained the supervisor of Sacred Heart EMS. Four months ago, Byron had come upon Rutherford in the break room with a girl that might have been twelve or twenty, it was impossible to tell. As he walked through the door, Rutherford tried to put something in his pocket. In his haste, he spilled it on the floor. A small pill rolled across the floor and came to rest against Byron's boot. He picked it up, and then looked at Rutherford.

Byron's voice was quiet, almost sinuous. "Oxy's, Don? What the hell are you doing with a pocketful of Oxy's?"

Rutherford made a small, scared sound in his throat. The girl, not liking the way things were unfolding, took off so fast it was hard to tell she had just been standing there. Byron and Rutherford stood looking at each other across the break room.

"C'mon Ram," Rutherford said, "It's just a little extra, man. Suzy's in college now and I swear to Christ, she costs more now than she did at home."

Byron looked at the pill in his hand. It was an Oxycontin, a very powerful pain medication. Several batches of the stuff had disappeared from the pharmacy in the last few months. It appeared that Byron had discovered where it had gone.

Rutherford spoke again.

"What do you say, Ram? I'll cut you in, man, no sweat. You know, just kind of keep this between us, huh?" He was almost whining.

Byron hurled the pill at Rutherford, who instinctively caught it.

"I don't give a fuck what you do in your spare time, Don. You get caught, it's your ass. Two things, though. One, you are, as of right now, officially off my back. I come in here naked with a kielbasa stuck up my ass, you just smile and say, 'Well, you have yourself a good shift, Ram'. Two, I get one run, *one* fucking run that somebody has overdosed on this shit and I find out it came from you, you're done. Got that?"

"Sure, Ram, no sweat, man. It's cool. I only sell 'em to folks from upstate. Keeps it away from me, right? So, we're good, then? Still friends?"

Byron laughed. "We were never friends, you fat, bald fuck. You've been looking for a reason to give me my walking papers since my divorce. Talking all that shit about how I must have really been a total bastard to make that sweet Samantha want to divorce me. You think I didn't know? That I wouldn't hear? It's a small hospital, Don, in a small town. Did you honestly think I wouldn't find out about the Christmas party? Sam told me all about how you tried to grab her tits, how you invited her back to your office. The only thing that kept me from stomping your ass was Sam. She begged me not to; afraid I'd lose my job. After the divorce, I didn't much care about it, one way or the other. Well, now I've got an insurance policy for my continued employment here. So you just keep on playing the Big Boss. Just steer clear of me. If I see too much of you, I'm liable to get to thinking about you trying to fuck my wife. You don't want me to think about that, Don. Believe me when I say that's the last thing you want. As a matter of fact, I'm starting to think about it right now."

Rutherford turned without a word and walked out of the break room. Since then he and Byron had walked circles around each other. That suited Byron to the ground.

Byron was still lying in bed thinking about the look on Rutherford's face when he had realized that Byron knew about his attempt to have sex with Sammy twenty minutes later, making him now officially eight minutes late for work. With a short laugh, he got up and started getting ready for work. He walked into the bathroom, flipping on the overhead light. His bathroom, like the whole trailer, was cramped, small, and dark. Even at noon, barely enough light made its way into the trailer to be considered gloom. He stared into the cracked and water-spotted mirror, taking inventory of the man looking back. Hair, mussed. Eyes, bloodshot and watery. Stress wrinkles radiated out from the corners of them like spikes of a smashed windshield. His jaw and neck were covered in several days' growth of stubble. When he spoke, he hardly recognized his own voice.

"Byron Lyndon Williamson, you look, to be blunt, like shit."

"You got *that* right, son."

Byron whipped around, his heart slamming dully in his temples. The voice had come from just over his left shoulder. Instinctively, he brought his arm up, fist cocked and ready.

There was no one there.

Byron slumped back against the basin, trying to catch his breath. After a few moments, when it seemed he wasn't going to have a heart attack just yet, he opened his eyes. He walked back into his bedroom and looked around. Nothing there. He looked in the closet, behind the door, even under the bed. Nothing. He spent several minutes walking through the small trailer, making sure he was alone. By the time he got back to the bathroom, he was beginning to wonder if he'd heard anything at all. *It was the vodka*, he thought. When people that aren't there begin commenting on your physical appearance, it was time to switch to beer. Byron was a practical man, if he was nothing else.

He began lathering his face, stopped, and decided just his neck would do. Hell with it, he thought, I think I'll grow a beard. He finished up in the bathroom and headed to the kitchen. Over a breakfast of Beanie Weenies and Coors Light, he looked over the day's paper. Nothing new or unusual there. Half the folks in the world were killing, raping, or just plain screwing the other half over. He put the paper down and looked over at the phone. It was time to call and check on the kids, but that entailed talking to Samantha. He had offered to pay for a second phone line, just for the kids, but Sam had refused. No sense in that, she had said. We have call waiting, and that's enough. With a heavy sigh, he reached for the phone and dialed the number. For a split second, as it began ringing, he was tempted to hang up and go on to work. He was actually taking the phone away from his ear when he heard Samantha's voice.

"Hello?"

"Hi, Sammy."

"Byron."

"Yeah. How are the babies?"

"You'd know if you saw them every now and then."

"Yes, Samantha, I know." A sigh.

"Of course, you're probably too busy, between the drinking and the job, right?"

Byron felt angler pulsing behind his eyes. *Not today, Sammy*, he thought. *Be fucked if I do this today. Besides, I'm drinking* on *the job, dammit. Killing two birds with one stone.*

"Sam, someone's got to pay the bills on the house you're living in. Someone's got to pay for the kid's doctor visits, dentist visits, Robbie's Little League equipment, your car... need I go on?"

"I told you I'd get a job. I'll pay my own way, and I'll take care of my kids. I don't need your help, and you damn well know it."

"They're not *your* kids! They're *our* kids! *FUCK*!"

"Stop shouting at me, Byron." The ice in her voice was cold enough to numb his ear.

"Sorry", he said, although he was nothing of the kind. "What are you going to do, Sammy? Huh? Work at Kmart? You think you can afford the house working for minimum wage?"

"I *told* you I wanted to go to school! I *told* you I should start taking classes! I *told* you I..."

"Sam", Byron said quietly.

"*What*, dammit?"

"I'm not doing this tonight. I'm not doing this. I refuse. You want to hate me, fine. You want to blame me for every lousy thing that has happened since we got married, fine. You can even blame me for giving Liza the genes that gave her the double-fucked leukemia, fine.

That's bullshit, but I can't stop you from thinking it. But I will *not* sit here and listen to this same old record. I won't. I want to talk to my children. That's all I want to do. Now, are you going to refuse to let me talk to them? Because if you are, so help me Christ, I will be over there with a Deputy Sheriff so fast your fucking head will spin."

"You *bastard*. You want to ruin your children's lives like you ruined mine, go right ahead."

The phone slammed down on the table, and Byron could see her stalking down the hall way to the living room where the kids would be watching Teletubbies. He sat back in his chair, leaning his head back with his eyes closed. He blew out a harsh breath. *Oh, man, you could've handled that so much better than that*, he thought. *So much better.*

A few moments later, he heard the phone pick up.

"Hello?"

Byron smiled.

"Hiya, Big Fella! How ya doing tonight?"

"Daddy! Where are you? Are you coming to get me?"

"No, bub, not tonight. Daddy has to go to work. I'll will come and get you on Saturday, okay? We'll go fishing at the river, how does that sound?"

"Liza too?"

"Sure, of course Liza can come, if she feels up to it. We'll slay some monster cats. Sound like a winner?"

"Sure, Daddy! That would kick ass!"

"Don't say that."

"Sorry, Daddy."

"Let me talk to Liza, Big Fella."

"'Kay, Daddy, I love you."

"I love you, too bub. Very much."

The phone clunked back down for a few seconds, and then Liza was there. Her soft voice always broke his heart. She was so tiny, so small for her age. Like a porcelain doll. As always, when she spoke, it was a battle to keep from weeping.

"Hi, Daddy."

Byron swallowed what felt like a lump of iron.

"Hi, Baby Girl. How's my angel tonight?"

"Fine." So *soft*.

"How are you feeling?"

"I'm fine. Legs hurt me."

"Have Mommy soak them tonight, okay? Soak them, and then lay on the heating pad for a while."

"Okay, Daddy, I will." She sounded so tired.

"Daddy loves you so much, Liza. I think about you every day, all day. I've got the picture you drew of the unicorn on the fridge, I'm looking at it right now."

"Love you, too, Daddy. You's going to see me morrow or next day?"

"Yes, baby. Daddy is coming to get you on Saturday, okay? You and me and the Bobbster are going down to the lake and catch a fish bigger than you are."

Liza laughed.

"No fishies bigger'n me, Daddy."

"You bet there are. Bigger than Daddy, some of them."

"Bigger'n Daddy? *Really*?" She sounded awe-struck.

"Yep, but I think we'll stick to the ones your size, okay?"

"Okay, Daddy. Love you."

"I love you, too Liza. You have sweet dreams in the night, okay?"

"You, too, Daddy. Bye."

"Bye, baby."

The phone made a muffled noise as Liza handed it to her mother.

"Sam, I just want to..."

Click.

The hum of the dead line burned his ear. He looked at the phone for a while, and then returned it to the cradle. He went to the fridge and got himself another Coors. He sat back down at the kitchen table and put his head on his arms. Then kitchen was quiet, save the sound of the ticking clock and the muffled sobs.

Chapter Four

Robbie and Liza sat in front of the television in the living room, watching Teletubbies. Well, *Liza* watched them, anyway. In Robbie's opinion, the Teletubbies were just about the most stupid thing on TV, possibly with the exception of Dora the Explorer. He wasn't a big fan of either one, but Liza loved them, and Robbie loved Liza, so there you go. It wasn't easy to be the big brother sometimes, but Robbie didn't mind. He had always felt very protective of Liza, even though he sometimes found himself hating the attention she received. He was a good boy at heart, though, and understood that the attention she was always getting was horrible.

He watched her now, as she stared raptly at the goofy, multicolored creatures on the screen. They didn't even speak *English*, for gosh sakes. They just made weird noises at each other. What was a kid supposed to learn from *that?* Well, to be fair, Dora the Explorer spoke Spanish a bunch of the time, but at least that was a *real* language. Robbie had heard some of the men that worked painting the hospital where his dad worked speaking it, so at least there was a reason for Dora to teach kids how to talk in Spanish. If Robbie ever met a giant, purple furry animal that made crazy noises at him, he would hit it on the head with his little league bat and run like hell.

Robbie sat looking blankly at the TV screen and thought about his mom and dad. All they ever did was fight, even on the phone. Fighting on the phone was probably the stupidest thing in the world, in Robbie's opinion. Even more stupid than the Teletubbies. Every time his mom and dad talked on the phone, his mom would end up in her bedroom, sitting on the bed and flicking through the channels on her TV so fast that you couldn't even see what was on. She was very angry for about an hour after each call, and Robbie and Liza had learned the best thing to do was to avoid her for that hour unless it was really important. Samantha didn't yell at them, but you could tell that she was really close to it, so it was better to just stay in the living room and wait it out.

Robbie was startled out of his thoughts by Liza's small voice.

"Bubby, why does Mommy 'n Daddy all the time fights?"

Robbie put his arm around Liza's tiny shoulders. He did it carefully, because she was usually very tender all over. He smiled at her and said, "Sis, I don't know. They fight because they can't get along, I guess. That's why most everybody fights."

Liza looked into his eyes and asked "They don't fights cuz of me, does they?"

Robbie was surprised. "No, Liza! Of course they don't fight because of you! Why would you think that? Mom and Dad love you and me better 'n anything."

She shrugged, the motion causing a small grimace of pain to flit across her face. "I was just thinkin' that they maybe fights cuz of where I's sick all the time. Maybe they wished they'd have another little girl that didn't hurted all the time and cried."

Robbie very carefully folded his baby sister into his arms.

"No, Sissy, that' not it at all. You can't help being sick. And Mommy and Daddy know that. They wouldn't want any other little girl in the world but you. You're their onliest one, and they love you more than anything."

"More than the Tubbies?"

Robbie laughed. "*Way* more than the Teletubbies. Truckloads more than the Teletubbies. 'Sides, who would love those furry goobers, anyway? They're just silly."

Liza put on an indignant face. "The Tubbies is sweet and nice and they loves *everybody*. I wish *I* live in Tubbie land. I bet I won't hurted if I lived in Tubbie land."

Robbie felt a wave of sadness wash over him. "No, Sissy, you probably wouldn't hurt if you lived in Teletubby land. But then, how would you know how to talk back to 'em? They can't talk right. You'd starve to death tryin' to ask for somethin' to eat, and they wouldn't know what you was even tryin' to say."

Liza smiled smugly at him. "The Tubbies would know zactly what I's sayin', cuz they's able to know what you's thinkin'."

Robbie thought for a minute. "Is that why they have those silly things on their heads? So they know what people are thinkin'?"

Liza nodded. "Yup. They's able to readed your *mind*."

"So, they're big and furry, they talk in a weird language, and they've got funny-shaped antennas on their heads… you know what, Liza-Bug?"

"What?"

"I think the Teletubbies are *aliens* from another planet. I think they're gonna invade the Earth and try to *eat* our *brains!*" He hooked his hands into claws and made gobbling noises on Liza's stomach. She giggled helplessly and slapped at his head. When she stopped laughing, they sat in silence watching the show for several minutes. Finally, she turned back to Robbie.

"So you sure that Mommy 'n Daddy ain't mad at me for bein' sick and cryin' all the time?"

Robbie reached over and planted a kiss on her forehead.

"I promise, Sissy. They ain't mad at you at all. And you know what? Even if they was, I'd just take you with me and we'd move to Disney World and live with Mickey Mouse at the Magic Castle. How would that be?"

Liza hugged her big brother as tightly as her little arms would let her.

"That would be the bestest. You are the bestest big Bubby in everywheres. I love you more than the Tubbies."

Robbie swallowed a lump in his throat, and for one terrifying second, he thought he was going to look like the biggest wussie on the planet by crying in front of his baby sister. He cleared his throat and hugged Liza back.

"I love you more than the Tubbies, too, Liza-Bug. Way more."

They sat that way, with their arms entwined, as the Teletubbies gave way to Dora and her backpack.

Chapter Five

Byron walked into the EMS staff room at seven thirty-four, eliciting an angry glance from Tiffany Brown. She'd been at Sacred Heart since it was built, if you believed the rumors, and felt that punctuality was the cornerstone of a well-rounded day. Byron ignored her gaze, and walked over to the coffee pot. As he poured himself a cup, Jack Blaire walked in.

"Hey, Ram! How goes it?"

"'Bout the same, Jack. How you doing?"

"Same ol', same ol'. Looks like we got the shit tonight. First of the month, baby. You know what that means. They're gonna come crawling outta the woodwork tonight, government checks at the ready. I bet we get multiple codes tonight, whattaya think?"

"Probably, Jack. Our tax dollars at work, man. Makes you proud to be an American, doesn't it?"

"Yeah. You know, I was thinking about that. In a sense, since we pay the taxes that make up those checks, *we're* paying the patients to take *them* to the hospital. Jacked up, huh?"

"That's too deep for me to even consider, Jack. Once again, you've left me with jaw agape with your burning perception of the state of our sad race."

Jack smiled a bit dazedly. He was never sure if Ram was making fun of him when he talked like that.

"Well, Cap'n, you ready to save the world?"

"Lead on, Jack. Stalwart hearts, and all that shit."

As they headed out to the service station to top off their tanks and service the unit, it began to rain. An intermittent drizzle became a slow, steady downfall, and by nine o'clock that night, a dense fog began to creep out of the river and across the town. Visibility was down to several yards.

"Gonna be one whole helluva lot of wrecks tonight if it keeps this shit up", said Jack.

Byron glanced up from his new Terry Brooks novel and looked out the windshield. The street lights played crazily across the glass as the wipers fought a vain battle to clear the rain away.

"Yeah, probably so. I guess that's why they pay us the big bucks."

Jack looked over at Byron. His partner was pale, paler than was usual. Dark circles covered his eye sockets, giving him a skull-like appearance. The new beard growth was actually striking, with an abundance of colors shooting through it. The most striking was the solid white standing out here and there in the thick facial hair. Byron was holding his book with one hand, his other nervously tapping the window glass with no particular rhythm. Jack screwed up his courage and, prepared for the backlash he was sure to get, asked Byron if he was all right. To his surprise, Ram just put his book in his lap and looked at him calmly.

"No, Jack, I don't think I am. I really don't."

Byron stared at his hands, trying to form his thoughts. After a moment, he looked back up.

"Man, I thought I was on top of this whole divorce thing, but every time I turn around, it bites me on the ass from a different angle. I get my bearings; get to thinking straight, then boom! Something happens. Like day before yesterday. I went shopping over to Kroger's, just pick up some shit, you know. Milk, bread, that kind of stuff. So here I am in the dairy section, trying to decide between two percent and whole milk, and all of the sudden I'm thinking about the time Bobby went tearing down the aisle, screaming about chocolate milk and tripped a stocker with his arms full of cheese slices. Jesus, Sammie was *mad*. I'm standin' there, thinking about that, and I notice an old woman staring at me. Then I realize that I'm crying. *Weeping*, man. Just standing in the middle of fucking Kroger's crying like a baby. What the hell is up with that? Christ."

"Have you given any thought about talking to Father Bern?" asked Jack, "I mean, that's what he's there for, Ram."

Father Daniel Bern was the resident priest at Sacred Heart. He was a tough old bastard that told it like it was. Byron liked him fine, but having a priest tell him that life was hard, get over it, wasn't his idea of help. Besides which, Byron had never felt that pouring your heart out to a man you barely knew would solve anything in any real way. Talking to priests, or shrinks for that matter, was a waste of time. After you "got it off your chest" it was supposed to be like some lanced boil in your soul, leaving you clear to heal. In Byron's opinion, that was bullshit. Talking about something did nothing to change that thing. It was what it was, end of story, and pissing and moaning about it wouldn't do anyone any good in the end. When he spoke again, his voice was dismissive.

"Nah, I don't think I need to involve....*SWEET JESUS CHRIST, LOOK OUT, JACK!!!*"

Jack jerked his eyes back to the road. Byron reached across him and jerked the steering wheel hard right. The ambulance skittered across the wet road on its left tires, and for one horrifying second, Jack was sure it was going to roll. Just as the unit was about to topple, gravity reasserted itself, and the ambulance ground to a screaming halt halfway on the median.

"What the *FUCK*, Ram?!?" Jack screamed. "Have you lost your fucking mind???"

Jack turned back to Byron, but he was screaming at an empty seat. Byron had jumped out of the unit before it had come to a complete stop and was now tearing back down the road behind them. Jack got out slowly, checking himself for injuries. Other than a slight ache across his chest where the seatbelt had nailed him, and a fear that he might have pissed himself, he appeared to be okay. He turned back to Byron who was now standing beside the road, peering into the curtain of rain. Blaire walked slowly towards him.

"Hey, Ram, what the hell, man? What was it?"

Byron turned back towards Jack, an incredulous look in his eye.

"What do you mean, 'what was it?'. Didn't you see them? They were standing in the middle of the road, for fuck's sake!"

Jack took a hesitant step back from Byron. Ram had a wild look in his eye, a look that Jack didn't care for in the least.

"Dude, there wasn't anyone in the road. There wasn't anything there at all. I would have seen somebody in the road, even in this soup."

"Jack, are you going to stand there and tell me that you didn't see those little girls in the road? Three of 'em, all in a row. Looked like they were going to church, or some shit. Jesus! They were standing right...fucking...*here*!"

Jack wiped the rain from his face. He was almost calmed down from the near-accident, and decided to give Ram a chance to explain.

Hell, maybe he *didn't* see them, the fog was thick tonight. He walked over to the edge of the road, pulling out his Maglite. Byron had his out, as well, and they spent several minutes looking into the field that bordered the road.

"Pull the unit back here and get the spot light out", said Byron.

Jack backed the unit into place and a moment later a blazing light streaked out of the passenger window. The light played back and forth across the field for a while, and then switched off.

"What are you doing?" Byron yelled. "Turn the light back on!"

Jack climbed out of the unit and walked back to where Byron was standing.

"Well?" asked Byron. "What is it?"

Jack slowly shook his head. Without a word, he shined his Maglite at the ground at Byron's feet.

"Where are the tracks, Ram?"

"*What?*"

"The tracks. Look at that field. You couldn't take two steps into that shit without being buried up to your ankles. Look."

Jack reached out with his toe and pressed the thick, clayey mud. It squirted up around his boot instantly.

"Where are the tracks, man? If they were in the road, they could have only gone two ways: into that field, or under our truck. I don't remember hitting anything, so they must have hauled ass into the field, right? So, where are they? Even if they just kept on running across the field, their tracks would be everywhere, wouldn't they? There aren't any tracks because they weren't *there*, Ram. There wasn't anyone in the road, man."

Byron screwed his fists into his temples. He stood like that, head down, for a very long time. When he looked up, a sad hope gleamed in his eyes.

"They were little girls, Jack. Probably didn't weigh anything. You know how little girls are. A strong puff of wind could blow them away, right? They didn't leave any tracks 'cause they didn't weigh hardly anything, right?"

Jack shook his head. This was it, he decided. Even if it meant losing his job, this was absolutely the last shift he was working with Byron Williamson. Fuck it, he thought, there are other jobs. Anything would be better than this shit. Ram wasn't going to quit until he got someone killed, and Jack wasn't going to stick around for that. To Byron, he said:

"Sure, Ram, that was it, man. No doubt. Little girls don't weigh shit. Well, they're gone, probably home by now, giggling about this whole thing. What do you say we head back to Sacred, get us some java?"

Byron nodded dumbly, and began walking back to the ambulance. When he walked right past it, Jack gently took him by the arm and led him back to his seat. The rain fell on, the crackle on the unit's roof sounding like the background static on an old television.

Chapter Six

Byron sat in the EMS room, drinking coffee. He had just been informed by his number-one favorite person in all the world that Jack Blaire had just given his notice. Either Jack got a new partner, or he no longer worked at Sacred. Don Rutherford couldn't keep the smug grin from surfacing on his face as he relayed this information to Byron. It remained there, pulling at his lips, until Byron turned calmly to him and stared at him for several moments. Unable to bear his gaze, Rutherford walked out of the room in what he was sure looked like a stalk, but in reality looked like what could only charitably called a slink.

Byron had felt a moment of blind rage, and thought seriously about finding Jack and putting him in intensive care. Then the feeling was gone, as quickly as it had come. Jesus, he couldn't blame Jack. When you start hearing voices and seeing imaginary little girls in the road, you sort of had to give up any anger you might be feeling at anyone else around you. Jack had every right to demand a new partner. Byron would have, had the situation been reversed. Probably one whole hell of a lot sooner, to boot. *Fuck it*, thought Byron, *I'm getting the hell out of here.*

He stood and walked towards the door. He had made it halfway there when Amber Jennson walked in. Amber had been the one constant in Byron's life through the tumultuous months since Liza's diagnosis. She was deeply in love with Byron, and had been since high school. She wasn't spiteful or vindictive about it, going so far as to help Sam plan their wedding. Amber was a registered nurse at Sacred, working the 7-to7 night shift. She was always there when Byron got to work, filling out charts and checking day shift's med counts. Byron smiled in spite of himself. It was always a good thing to see Amber. She seemed to dispel some of the grayness that hung over his life like a pall. The smile faltered once he saw the expression on her face. He knew what she was going to say before she said it, and mentally screamed at her not to say it, not to implicate herself in this insanity.

"Hey, Byron. How's my boy doing tonight?"

He smiled weakly at her. He couldn't lie to her, and he knew it. He had never been able to lie to Amber, ever since they were kids back in high school. She had always been able to see right through him, like she came equipped with Byron Williamson X-Ray goggles.

"I've been better Amber. I guess you heard, huh?"

She smiled at him. "Yeah, I may have heard something. You want to talk about it?"

Byron just stood there for a minute, thinking. *Why not*, he thought. *What the hell could it hurt to tell Amber? She's not a priest or a damn shrink, she's a friend.* He looked at her, his mouth set in a grim line.

"Okay, Amber. Here's the deal: I'm drinking too much, not sleeping enough, hearing voices in my head, seeing people that aren't there, my marriage is utterly and completely over, and my little girl is dying. I think that just about sums it up." And then as if a mental levee had burst, he began to weep, his chest hitching and air tearing out of his mouth in little gasps.

Amber immediately reached out for him and took him in her arms. She led him to the EMS room, then closed and locked the door behind them. Putting her arms around his neck, she whispered, "Now. Just let it come. Let it out. I'm here, and I've got you."

Byron spent almost a half an hour going thoroughly to pieces. The loud, braying sobs tapered off into a fine trembling that ran through his body like a live wire. After what seemed to him like an eternity, he was able to stand back and look Amber in the face. Her scrub top was light blue, and he had wept it dark on her shoulder. He suddenly sat down, as if all the strength had gone out of his legs. Amber sat next to him, holding one of his hands in both of hers.

"Well," he said, "What do you think? Time for the padded cell yet?" He smiled weakly at her, trying to take the edge off his voice.

"No, I think we can hold off on the padded cell just a *bit* longer," she replied with a sad smile. "You're not ready for a psych ward just yet, but there is something most definitely has to be done about this. You can't go on this way, you know."

"I know," he said. "I just don't know what the hell to *do*. I mean, those kids in the road, there were *there*, Amber. I *saw* them, just as clearly as I'm seeing you right now. Three little girls, all in a row, all even dressed the same. They were wearing these…"

Byron's voice faded and his eyes took on a far-off cast. Amber waited patiently beside him as he figured his way through this. After several minutes, Byron gave a lurch, and was up and halfway to the door before Amber even realized he was moving. He tore at the door handle, fumbling with the lock.

"Byron, honey, what is it?" she cried, her voice cracking with concern.

He managed to get the door unlocked and ripped it open, nearly taking it off the top hinge. His head whipped around and he looked at her. Amber fell back into the chair, instinctively recoiling from the terror she saw in his face.

"I won't go back there," he whispered. "Do you understand me? I *won't*. Not for you, not for anybody. That wasn't supposed to happen. It was an accident, they all said so. It was an accident, and we tried to help, and *I won't go BACK*!!!"

Byron spun around and ran out of the EMS room. Amber could hear the receding fall of his boots on the tile floor as he ran out of the back bay of the E.R. and into the night. Amber sat still, her hand convulsively pulling at the neck of her scrub top. Two tears slid slowly down her cheeks, adding more darkness to her damp top.

Chapter Seven

Byron spent the rest of that rainy night walking the streets of town. He had nowhere in particular to go, and was surprised more than once to find himself standing in front of his old house, watching his children through the front window. He walked back and forth across town, and up the winding road that led to the lake. He sat by the lakeside for a while, listening to the rain patter on the water's surface. He loved this place, this small town in Tennessee, hardly large enough to warrant a dot on a state map. He had traveled halfway around the world, seen and done things the people of this town had only seen on TV, and yet it was here that his mind had kept returning during his absence.

All through Basic Training, while the Drill Instructors were screaming and chaos was completely encompassing every waking second of his day, he could still find the quite place in his mind that whispered *home*. When every movement of his day had been planned for him, and spare time was a myth, only heard of and never seen, he could be transported in an instant to this place. It was so real in his mind that he would often come back to himself in the barracks and still smell the pine, with one of the D. I.'s bellowing in his face about what a complete fuck-up he was.

His time in Iraq had been eventful, to say the least. But even there, with the sand cutting into every crevice on his body and the heat a physical entity wrapping his body like a gauze, Dawkin's Mill was never more than a thought away.

He hadn't had many close friends growing up here. It wasn't that he was antisocial, or that he was difficult to get along with. Quite the opposite, in fact. There had often been times that Byron had felt that this boy or that one was getting too close, that the bonds of a true friendship were beginning to tighten. When this happened, he simply broke off contact with that particular boy. Not enough to cause hurt feelings, just enough to keep the relationship from growing any stronger.

His parents had noticed this pattern, especially his mother, and were for a while both worried that Byron might be having some sort of difficulty. They worried needlessly, because Byron was as fit mentally as his body was physically. He was not xenophobic in the least. Byron quite simply didn't need anyone else in his life. Or, to be more precise, he didn't need anyone else to share his exploration and enjoyment of Dawkin's Mill.

It was actually a selfish desire to keep all the hidden trails and caves that he found in the woods around town to himself, and he knew it. Once, he came upon a small waterfall that hid an almost perfectly round cave at its base. Although the water rushed by not feet away, the cave was not a bit damp. Byron discovered the reason for this when he camped there one night. He built a small fire, watching that the smoke didn't become too dense and choke him out. To his happy surprise, the smoke rose straight up to the roof of the cave, where it dissipated through several small cracks. He built his fire up larger, and then climbed up the hill beside the waterfall. He looked on in glee as smoke rose like fog from the myriad of tree roots that covered the ground above the cave.

It was the perfect camp, something right out of an old west movie or a pirate's keep. To Byron, every time he entered the cave he felt he had become one of the Lost Boys, needing only Tinkerbell to cinch the whole deal. The cave could have been a base from which Byron and a gang of boys could have ran amok, their yells and laughter echoing across the hills.

But Byron wanted to keep the cave just as it was, so he told no one about it. There were dozens of other such places he had found over the years in his rambling, and all but one remained known only to Byron. On the one occasion that he returned to one of his many haunts and found it full of drunken teen-age boys, he had merely watched from the shadows as they made fools of themselves. The boys had never known that Byron had been there, although on several occasions, he could have reached out and touched any one of them.

Byron never went back to that place again.

It was simply how he was. He was at home in the gentle woods around his home, and needed nothing but the wind in the trees and his own company to make him sublimely happy.

After his parents had figured out that their son wasn't gearing up to be the next Ted Bundy, they stepped back and let the boy run. Occasionally, Patricia would mention that it wouldn't kill Byron to have a friend over every now and then, but for the most part, the three of them were a very harmonious family. There was of course the occasional disagreement, but Byron felt that his family was just right. They needed and steered clear of each other in exactly the right mixture, something that Byron only truly appreciated many years later when he had seen how other families interacted.

Coming out of the haze of memories, Byron realized he had walked all night. He was soaked through, and by then there was discernable light cutting through the fog in the east. He had decided that it was time to head for home. He arrived at his run-down single wide just as the sun poked its head through the low-lying eastern cloud cover. As he stood on the crumbling concrete steps that led up to his front door, he felt the warming rays play across his face. His closed eyes had patterns of orange-red sunlight dappled across them. For just one moment, he could honestly believe that everything was going to be all right. Then the sun fell behind the clouds, and his life draped its harshness over him like a heavy blanket again. He suddenly rememberd that, having walked home, his truck was at the hospital. If they could find anyone willing to run with him, they would have to come pick him up in an ambulance. *Damn.* He sighed, and then turned the key in his lock and let himself inside.

The furniture was mostly cast-off and second hand stuff, the sort of furniture you find at yard sales that makes you wonder why in God's name the people hadn't just burned the things in the first place. The few wall hangings were scattered throughout the house, and most of these consisted of drawings done by his children. The dishes in the sink were beginning to cultivate enough mold that a new civilization could spring up at any moment, and the trash was sitting all along the back wall of his kitchen. He had meant to take it out on numerous occasions, but it always seemed that something had been more important at the time. Looking at the swill now, he realized that it wasn't more important duties that kept him from cleaning up this sty; it was a very bad case of him not giving enough of a damn to bother.

Byron closed the flimsy door behind him. (He still couldn't figure out why he bothered locking it, a two year-old could have broken through it with a plastic shovel.) He slumped his way to the couch and fell onto it with a grunt. A small dervish of dust flew up from around his ass, and he coughed. He began the process of stripping of last night's uniform, throwing his mud-covered boots and B.D.U. pants into the corner. *I've got to do some laundry,* he thought, *I'm down to wearing the same nasty shit I've had on for weeks.* He then laughed to himself. Like he was going to jump right up and head to the laundry mat today. Somehow, the cleanliness of his clothing had taken a back seat to the rest of his problems of late. His grooming standards had taken a serious hit.

He leaned back into the couch, letting his head rest on the back and closing his eyes. He was beyond exhausted, he knew, but there was little hope of getting any real sleep today. His limbs sluggish with fatigue, he made his way into the kitchen to find something to quiet the howling in his stomach. He opened the refrigerator door and stood looking with melancholy eyes at the contents. There was a half a can of pork and beans, a moldy Tupperware bowl of months-old spaghetti, nothing that a man would truly *want* to eat, short of starvation. He shrugged and got a can of Coors. At least the beer wouldn't be moldy, he hoped. Liquid bread. Taking his can back into the living room, Byron once more sat down on the threadbare couch. He flipped on the television, but nothing seemed to be worth watching. The canned laughter sounded like the desperate, fear-driven shrieks of the recently mad. Thumbing the mute button, he sat and sipped his beer while staring blankly at the screen before him. His eyes grew heavy, and the beer can began to slide from his loosening hand. *What do you know*, he thought groggily, *I'm actually going to be able to slee…*

His eyes slid closed.

Chapter Eight

Byron opened his eyes and squinted into the harsh desert sun. His Kevlar helmet was beginning to smell like a used sock drawer in high summer. He mopped his face off with his bandanna and took another look out of the Humvee. His vehicle was the fourth one back, just behind the convoy commander's. Theirs was an eight-vehicle convoy, part of a large body of troops moving from Baghdad to Fallujah. The 3rd Infantry Division was the first Allied force to cross the border into Iraq, and had just finished taking Baghdad in early April. The 1st Brigade captured Saddam International Airport and immediately re-christened it Baghdad International Airport. That little adventure won the 3rd Division its first Medal of Honor since the Korean War, awarded to Sergeant First Class Paul Ray Smith.

2nd Brigade got their own fifteen minutes of fame with the much over-publicized (in Byron's opinion) "Thunder Run" into downtown Baghdad. Although Byron felt like he and the boys of the 2nd were being treated a bit too much like rock stars, he had to admit it wasn't an altogether bad feeling to be rolling through downtown

Baghdad like they owned the place. After their action in Baghdad, the 3rd Infantry Division was re-tasked with the occupation of Fallujah. There had been some bad blood there between U.S. forces and local protestors, with several incidents involving the shooting deaths of the protestors. 3rd Armored Cav was being replaced by the boys of the 2nd Brigade. The men of the 2nd had been warned that the climate in Fallujah was becoming decidedly unfriendly to the American presence there, and that they were to watch their ass. Byron figured they needed to be told that just about as badly as they needed vital intelligence as to which way the sun was going to come up in the morning, but what the hell, they *were* at war here, right?

As they rolled into the outskirts of Fallujah, just behind Byron's Humvee was the Aid and Litter team and the alternate LZ team. Behind that was the recovery vehicle and there was a gun truck bringing up the rear. In front of the convoy commander was the primary LZ team and the lead gun truck. Byron's placement as Combat Life Saver/ Medic ensured him a place near the middle of the convoy, so he could respond quickly to any casualties that occurred at either end of the convoy.

He shared the space inside his Humvee with the five-man team he was part of. The driver, Private Sam Nichols, was a young kid from West Virginia, and seemed to have an endless supply of dirty jokes. It was his job to keep them moving, no matter what. In the passenger seat was First Sergeant Max Fleming, who was very intense during these convoys, a marked difference to the sunny, laid-back approach to life he had back at base. Directly behind the First Sergeant sat Byron, who at that time was a Sergeant. Next to him in the driver's side passenger seat was a Specialist named Kevin McDonald. McDonald was a quiet, reserved man who had a reputation for dependability, especially in a firefight.

Standing in the turret, manning the .50 caliber heavy machine gun, was Private Matthew Henderson, who was (at least in Byron's humble opinion), a complete idiot that shouldn't be trusted with Silly Putty, let alone a high-caliber automatic weapon. Apparently the Army thought differently, because there he stood, his eyes traversing the land around them constantly.

Byron didn't know what it was exactly that made him so nervous about Henderson. The man was well enough liked by the other men in the unit, but there was something about his eyes that left Byron feeling just slightly disconcerted whenever he looked into them. There was something in them that caused Byron to adopt a defensive position instantly. Maybe it was the way Henderson always seemed to look *through* you instead of *at* you. Whatever it was, Byron would have felt much better had Henderson been assigned to one of the other Humvees. Hell, assigned to another *unit*, come to that.

The war had seemed like some sort of walking dream to Byron. The carnage was real, as was the blood, and the first time a round had slapped into the side of the Humvee he had been standing beside, he had sent a short, pressurized jet of urine into the pants of his ACUs.

There were moments of pure, unadulterated terror, but these were off-set by long, grinding days of unabated boredom. He had done his duty, and, according to his commanding officer, had done so superbly.

It wasn't that he didn't feel pure terror when the bullets were streaking back and across the sky, tracers arcing lazily through the hot, dry air. He *was* terrified. It was just that, in some odd way, he was like he was terrified for someone else. It was if the fear that should have sent massive amounts of adrenaline into his system never appeared. He walked from casualty to casualty without haste, without any attempt to avoid incoming fire at all. This caused a great deal of talk around the base about what a cold, methodical son of a bitch Williamson was. He would have loved to explain to the other men that being "cold" had nothing to do with it. However, he was unable to find a way to convey to them the feeling that this whole war appeared to be happening to someone else, and that he was merely watching it from afar, as if on a big screen television with incredible clarity.

Although he couldn't understand why he felt as he did about combat, he was grateful for it. He had seen men that he knew personally to be some of the meanest human beings on the planet cower in a hastily dug fighting pit with their weapons lying on the ground at their feet and their hands wrapped around their Kevlar helmets, screaming like children. Mercifully, there were very few such instances. In the majority of the cases, the men in the 3rd were doing their duty in a business-like fashion, accepting the incoming rounds and dull thumps of mortar fire, and then carrying on anyway.

There had been far fewer full-on engagements than Byron had expected. While he had no images of World War Two-type battles being fought, he had assumed that there would have been more "army-on-army" fights. Instead, they had found themselves fighting a constant running battle, with retreating Iraqi troops stopping just long enough to give them harassment fire, and then falling back rapidly. That's not to say there were no real fights; there had been plenty of those. As the medic, Byron had gotten to see the results of those far more than he had desired to.

Small-arms fire does horrible things to the human body at close range, but when you add fragmentation munitions into the mix, well, the bodies stop even *resembling* anything human. Pieces of bodies are flung about like a careless child's toys. The truly terrible part of it all was how hard it was for some people to die. Cataclysmic systemic damage, large sections of their body lying feet and even yards away, and yet they could find within them the strength to scream so loudly that it was a miracle that their vocal cords didn't simply explode under the strain. In one nightmarish encounter, Byron found himself helplessly trying to tell an Iraqi soldier that he would be all right, just calm down, when the soldier's entire lower body was laying in the dirt on the far side of a small square in a town the name of which Byron could no longer even remember.

The Iraqi had grasped Byron's hands in his own, talking in a non-stop stream of Arabic that Byron could not even begin to translate. Nor could the Iraqi understand any of Byron's comforting

English. Byron had felt so torn inside, kneeling at the side of a man that had moments ago been his mortal enemy, an enemy that was rapidly painting the hard-packed dirt under them in scarlet.

This man was dying a truly horrible death, and there wasn't even anyone there to whom he could give his last words. Was he asking Byron to give his love to his wife and children? Was he cursing Byron and wishing that Byron would join him in death in this filthy street? Who knows? The man had shivered violently several times, and then Byron watched as his pupils dilated and listened to the whoosh of his last tidal breath. That was it, the end. Byron rose from the dead man and went over to help another casualty.

Throughout the rest of that day, and for many, many nights that followed, the dying Iraqi's last words haunted Byron. He began to obsess about it. He found one of the interpreters in the unit and tried his best to repeat back what the man had said to him, but the interpreter just shrugged and told Byron that it sounded like gibberish to him.

Byron was saved the pain of a drawn-out introspection when First Sergeant Fleming, who had been watching Byron in that spooky way sergeants have of keeping tabs on their soldiers without their knowledge, walked up to him and placed a warm, comforting hand on his shoulder.

"I understand that you had a spot of trouble out of that haji back there," he said. "Fucker gave you an earful, and you don't know what the hell he meant, is that about right?"

Byron was instantly excited. "Yeah, Sarge, that's exactly what happened. I asked the interpreter what the guy said, but you know those guys, half of them speak Arabic worse than they speak English. You have any idea what that guy was saying?"

Fleming leaned in close towards Byron, so close that the lips of their Kevlar helmets were nearly touching. With a look of great sincerity in his eyes, he said, "Yeah, I know what he said, son."

Byron was practically jumping from one foot to the other in his excitement. "What was it, Sarge? What the hell was he saying? Man, it's messing with me, not knowing what that cat was saying, but shit, I mean, I just felt like I should know what…"

Fleming shut down Byron's jabber with a short, brisk shake. Byron's head flopped back and forth hard enough to see stars. Once he was clear-headed enough to look Fleming in the eyes, the First Sergeant continued.

"There, that's a bit better. You were getting just a bit sideways on me there, soldier. Now, as to what that haji said, it's very simple. Are you listening closely?"

Byron's head nodded up and down, as solemn as a schoolboy.

Satisfied that he had Byron's complete attention, Fleming went on. "What that haji said back in that town is the exact same thing you, or me, or anyone else, for that matter, would have said if the situation had been reversed. He was simply telling you that his balls, and the legs that they were attached to, had just been blown across a market street. What the fuck did you think he was saying? 'Tell Mom I love her?' 'Don't forget to feed my dog?' 'I cheated on my fourth grade spelling test?' God-*damn*, Williamson, the bottom of his body had just parted ways with the top. Don't you think that might have been something that was lying pretty heavy on his mind at that moment? Jesus, son, use your damn head for something other than holding your goddamn helmet up every now and then, what do you say?"

Fleming turned and walked away. Byron stood there, transfixed for several minutes before he came to himself. With a look of perplexed amazement at his retreating First Sergeant's back, Byron gave a sickly-sounding chuckle, and headed back for his vehicle. That night he slept his four hours without a single dream.

The convoy was moving at a steady forty-five miles an hour, maintaining vehicle dispersion and keeping a close eye on the surrounding terrain. Most organized resistance had ended by this point, something that most Americans back home thought to be a grand thing. For the men on the ground in Iraq, most longed for the days of uniformed enemies standing before them. Now, the age of civilian-clothed snipers, suicide bombers, and I.E.D.s was coming to fruition.

Every pile of rubbish, every car sitting beside the road that hadn't been there the day before, every sandy patch beside the road could be an I.E.D. It made every ten-mile convoy feel like a hundred miles. The tension was constant, and there was no respite from the constant, nagging fear and the mind-numbing heat. Tempers were short, and the sleep-deprivation was not helping anything.

The men of the 3rd hadn't taken a shower for two weeks, and their clothing could just about get up and walk around by itself. The stench was something that a person acclimated to quickly, and Byron was amused when a reporter for CNN had stuck his head into their Humvee for a quick interview and had withdrawn rapidly, vomiting violently onto the side of the vehicle. Henderson had looked at the reporter with open hostility and said, "Now, motherfucker, clean that shit off my vehicle." The reporter, unsure whether Henderson was joking, tried a weak smile and mumbled something about not having brought his Windex with him. Henderson had to be physically restrained from exiting the Humvee and beating the reporter senseless. The reporter, realizing that discretion is the better part of valor, left quickly to find someone else to interview. This incident hadn't gone very far towards easing Byron's feelings of disquiet towards Henderson.

The convoy stopped on the outskirts of Fallujah proper, while the lead gun truck cleared the way forward. As the men sat sweltering in their vehicle, Byron noticed that Henderson was mumbling something to himself, over and over. Straining to hear, he could just make it out over the rumbling of the Humvee's engine.

"The fuck you lookin' at, you goddamn haji bitches? Huh? What's so fucking funny? You see something funny? The fuck you lookin' at?" Henderson was repeating this, his eyes locked on a group of Iraqi civilians standing on the street corner across from their vehicle. His voice was odd, flat and inflectionless. Byron was reaching up to pull on Henderson's ACU leg and ask him what the hell was wrong with him when a strident ringing filled the Humvee. He looked around, trying to locate the source of the sound. It wasn't any of the various warning bells of the vehicle itself, and none of their coms were keyed up. Reaching up to grab First Sergeant Fleming's shoulder, he asked "Sarge, what the hell is that?" Fleming turned to him and Byron fell back into his seat in shock. Fleming's eyes were gone, empty red-black holes where they had once been. He had a horrible smile on his face, and when he spoke, his voice sounded like breaking glass. "That's the phone, you fucking ineffective piece of shit. Don't you know anything?"

The sound reached a pitch that hurt Byron's ears. It felt like his brain was trying to run out of them. Fleming was turning, reaching across the seat towards Byron, his hands hooked into claws. "Answer the phone, you fucker, answer the phone. Answer the phone. ANSWER THE PHONE!!!! ANSWER THE..."

Chapter Nine

"phone, answer the phone, oh, God, answer the damn phone. Please, answer it, answer it before my head explodes, answer the phone…"

Byron jerked into a sitting position on the couch. He blinked owlishly around the dim living room. After several seconds of trying to make sense of his surroundings, he realized that the phone *was* ringing. He snatched it off the cradle and mumbled into it.

"H'lo? Whozat?"

"Byron? Byron, honey, are you awake?" Amber's voice cut through the fog of his dream and brought him back into the present with an almost audible *snap.*

"Yeah, Amber, I'm here. I must have dozed off. What's going on?" He glimpsed at the clock over the television, and was shocked to see he had been asleep for almost twelve hours. The sun had set, and the room was a dark cave.

Amber was silent for a second, and then made an odd, hiccupping sound. It took Byron a few seconds to realize that Amber was trying not to sob. His unease deepened.

"Amber, are you all right? Look, I'm sorry about running out on you last night, there was no excuse for that. I was just…"

"No, Byron, it's not that. It's just, well, you need to get over here to Sacred… it's… you need…"

Byron was beginning to feel panic latch onto his chest with tight arms. He took a deep breath, repeated it, and then spoke into the phone. He was amazed at how calm he sounded.

"Amber, you need to tell me what's going on. What happened? Has there been a mass causality or something? I don't have my radio with me, so I didn't hear any tones drop. Is it a school bus or something like that? What?"

Amber took a deep breath of her own. "No, Byron, nothing like that. It's Liza. You need to get over here. She…" Amber realized she was talking down a dead line. Byron had hung up after hearing the word "Liza". Amber hung up the phone and turned back to the nurse's desk. Once she got there, she got Liza's chart down and sat staring blankly at it. Byron would be here soon. Byron would know how to handle this. He *had* to.

Byron came through the E.R. doors so hard that he knocked one of them slightly off its track. He was breathing heavily, that ambulance ride he had hoped for to get back to the hospital never materializing, so he had run all the way. Without slowing, he made his way down the hallway to where he knew the pediatric bay was located. If it had been empty when Liza had arrived, they would have put her in there. And sure enough, standing outside the pediatric bay was Dr. Donald Rutherford, his arm comfortingly around Samantha's shoulders. He looked up and saw Byron, and guiltily lowered his arm. Then his face firmed up and he stepped between Byron and the bay door. This was a mistake. Rutherford opened his mouth and began, "Ram, it is my feeling that due to your drinking and other behaviors, that it would be detrimental to Elizabeth for you to see her at this time. If you would like to –*URCK!*"

This was as far as he got as Byron bodily lifted him several inches off the floor by the throat and flung him down the hallway. Rutherford hit the wall and slid down into a sitting position, a look of almost comic surprise on his face. Samantha gave a startled little yelp, and took a step back from Byron. He never even glanced at her as he went past. He entered the bay, and everything else went away. All he could see was Liza, lying on the hospital bed, tubes running out of her from all over her body. Monitors kept track of her heart rate, blood pressure, and oxygen saturation. Liza was mercifully unconscious. She lay like a doll, draped in white. Ram felt his heart fall into his boots. He walked toward the bed, his steps uneven and slow, like an old man.

"Liza, baby, daddy's here," he said in a voice that he didn't recognize as his own. "Daddy's here, and you're going to be fine. Tomorrow's Saturday, remember? You, me, and the Bobbster are going fishing tomorrow. So you have to get up so we can go, all right? You have to wake up now, baby. Liza? Honey, can you hear Daddy?"

From the bed came only the sounds of the machines that were keeping his little girl alive. Byron slid slowly down beside the bed, taking Liza's tiny hand in his own. He sat that way for a long time.

Chapter Ten

Rutherford was waiting on Byron when he finally came out of Liza's room. With his few remaining hairs plastered across his pate with sweat, he stared hard into Byron's eyes. The hatred was so strong in his eyes that Byron was surprised he couldn't hear them snapping, as if they were full of electricity.

"All right, you self-righteous son of a bitch," he began. "You've crossed the line this time. You physically assaulted me, with witnesses. I'll have you in jail for this. See how much time you spend with your daughter from the goddamned county lock-up!"

Byron looked over at Rutherford. Had he really ever given this tiny little man more than a passing thought? Had he *really*? What the hell had he been thinking? When he spoke, his voice was calm and neutral. "You want to call the cops, Don? Fine. Call them. If you don't want to use your private line to do it, I'll even give you the fifty cents to call them from the pay phone in the lobby. Once I'm taken into custody, I'm sure that the officer in charge and I will find all sorts of interesting things to discuss, don't you?"

Rutherford cut his eyes left and right. There was no one within earshot. He leaned in and fixed Byron with a smug smile. "Sure,

Williamson. I'm sure that you can find all *sorts* of things to talk about. I bet that you could give them a verbatim account of what happened with those fucking Oxy's, but you know what? Who the hell do you think they're going to believe? The man that just assaulted a doctor trying to treat a dying little girl, or some drunk medic that smells like he bathed about a year ago? Hmmm? Who do you think will come down on the good side of that particular conversation?" He leaned back, a well-pleased look on his face.

"Yeah, you're right, Don," said Byron. "It wouldn't look very good at all for me, would it? Matter of fact, I bet they would just write it off to me being vindictive and petty, trying to set you up. The thing is this, Don: I figured that you might get just a bit lax once you figured out that I wasn't going to blow the horn on you. I figured that you thought you had enough room between you and the idiots you sell that shit to that would keep you clean. So you know what *I* did, Don? *I* checked the batch numbers on the missing Oxycontin from here and had a friend of mine in the Kentucky State Police run a check. Come to find out several of the Oxy's from those batches were confiscated in a couple of drug raids. The only thing that the folks that got busted could say was that they had gotten their supply from a guy that had gotten *his* supply from a doctor in Tennessee. See how that works out, Don? Who has access to those medications? And of those people, who are doctors? It wouldn't take very fucking long at all for my buddy in the KSP to run a check that led him right to your door, especially if he was provided with just a little bit more information as to where those Oxy's may have originated."

Rutherford's pupils constricted with fear. "Bullshit," he said. "You're bluffing. There's no way that shit can be traced back to me."

Byron seemed to give it some thought. "Well, maybe not. Let me ask you one question, though: Those folks that got busted up in Kentucky, they said they got that shit from a guy that got it from a doctor. They even gave a description of the guy. Mid-twenties, skinny, dark hair and brown eyes. They said he was wearing a trucker's hat that said "David Allen C.E.O. on it. Like that cartoon on Adult Swim called Squidbillies, you know the one I'm talking about?"

Rutherford began shaking. "That son of a *bitch*," he muttered, "He swore he wouldn't sell anywhere *near* here. He swore he'd…" He seemed to remember that Byron was standing right in front of him. With a deep breath, he said, "Fine. We'll forget the whole thing happened. It never happened, all right? Does that suit you, you bastard?"

Byron was amused to see that Rutherford was almost crying. He was tempted to twist the knife just a little more, but then weariness descended on him like lead. "Fine, Don, it never happened. We're square on that. Now, what you do is take your fat little ass upstairs and get Liza a room in I.C.U., and then you get me the best oncologist we've got. Money is no object here, Don. Anything that my insurance doesn't cover, *you* will. Got it?"

Rutherford looked shocked. "That's fucking blackmail, pure and simple!"

Byron walked away. Over his shoulder, he replied, "Yes, Don, it is. Isn't karma a wonderful thing to see in action?"

<u>Chapter Eleven</u>

Liza's room in I.C.U. looked as much like a little girl's room as Byron and Samantha had been able to make it. There was only so much one could do with a hospital room, however, and what you wound up with was a hospital room that looked like it had been covered over with stuffed animals, balloons, and crayon drawings. In all, it just seemed to lend a sense of desperation to an already desperate situation.

Liza was swimming in and out of consciousness, the morphine drip attached to her I.V. keeping her from feeling the worst of the pain. When she was at herself enough for conversation, she asked if she could watch her Teletubbies DVD. The television in the room was not equipped with a DVD player, so Byron had gone straight out and bought one of the small DVD players that parents often get for their children to watch on long car rides. By the time he arrived back with it, Liza was once more deeply asleep, so he hooked the player up within easy reach of her, with the Teletubbies DVD ready to go at the push of a button.

Byron and Samantha had not grown closer throughout the last few days, but they had managed to find a way to occupy the same space without devolving into bitter recriminations against one another. This wasn't an ABC after-school special, as far as Byron was concerned, but at least it was a step in the right direction. Seeing Byron with Liza, and with Robbie when he was there, seemed to have a calming effect on Samantha. It was if she was reminded that yes, he *was* their father, and just maybe he *did* love them. Byron didn't care if it was that, or the vast quantities of Valium that Samantha was taking, just so long as they kept their armed truce in place.

The oncologist, a small Greek man named Pyrrus, had taken Byron and Samantha into his office and laid out for them in very stark terms what Liza's chances for survival were. Barring a miracle, which *has* been known to happen, he stressed, Liza would not last much longer. How long is much longer, Byron had demanded? A week, Pyrrus said, a month, maybe two. There was just no certainty, especially when the patient was a child. Children react in a totally different way than do adults, he said. Samantha had sat numbly, staring at an architectural picture of a Venetian piazza. That suited Byron. Although Samantha was not without intelligence, she was at heart a simple woman, and would not have known what questions to ask, or what the answers meant.

Many parents, upon discovering that their child has a disease or disorder, would spend vast amounts of time researching everything possible about it. Not Samantha. She had simply expected Byron to know everything there was to know about leukemia in children. *Like that's one of the first classes they gave me in Combat Life Saving, dammit,* he thought. Byron *had* read exhaustively about the disease, its progression, remission, symptoms, and treatments. All that knowledge now rolled around in his mind like so many useless boulders as his little girl lay busily dying a few rooms away.

Dr. Pyrrus ended his consultation with them by saying that it was important that they not wear themselves out. He suggested taking turns staying with Liza, so that each parent could grab a little sleep and clean up. This seemed like a fine idea to Byron, because deep down, he wasn't sure how much longer the truce between himself and Samantha was going to last. Probably as long as her Valium prescription did. He realized that was unfair, and chastised himself for it.

They left Dr. Pyrrus' office and headed down to the parking lot to figure out the schedule that they needed to make, to ensure that Liza would always have one or the other one of them there when she woke up. Liza had just been medicated, the charge nurse assured them, and would probably be asleep for several hours. Byron and Samantha decided to take this time to go to their respective homes, pack some clothing and other essentials, and take a much-needed nap.

As they arrived at Samantha's car, Byron turned to her and put his hand on her cheek. *Yes*, he thought, *part of me does still love her. God damn it all.* He looked her in the eyes and said, "Sammy, I'll go home and grab some gear and take the first watch. I'll call you if anything happens, okay? Go home and get some sleep. If nothing happens, I'll call you in the morning, and you can come and stay for a while. We'll take turns, like Dr. Pyrrus said, that way we aren't both worn out. You know you can't really rest in those hospital rooms. Once we get into a regular rhythm, one of us will always be with her. Okay?"

Sammy slowly reached up, and for a moment, Byron thought she was going to cup her hand over his on her cheek, the way she had done so many times over the years. Instead, in what seemed like slow motion, she pulled her hand back and let fly. Her palm slapped onto his face with a small, unimportant snapping sound. He felt no pain at all. He just stood there looking blankly at her. He hadn't even moved his hand from her cheek.

She raised her hand again, and this time Byron's reflexes took over. As her hand descended, he stepped slightly back and caught her hand in mid-flight. Samantha brought her other hand up, and Byron caught that one, too. He looked at her, trying to garner some sense from this outburst. She didn't struggle to free her hands from his, she just stood there.

In a small, dull voice, she said, "Take your hands off me. Never touch me again. Do you understand that? If you see me falling down a flight of stairs, you let me fall. Never touch me again."

"Sammy, what the *hell*..." Byron began.

"No," she said. "You're not listening. You do not touch me. You do not speak to me outside of that goddamn room my little girl is dying in, and even in there, you only speak to me about things that pertain directly to her. Do you understand that? Tell me you understand that, Byron. I need to hear you say it."

Byron's eyes darkened. In a dead voice, he told her he understood.

"Good," she said. "Now, get out of my way. You want the first deathwatch, it's all yours. I will be back here at eight in the morning, at which time, I expect you to kiss Liza good-bye and then fuck off until eight the following morning. Do you understand that?"

Byron said that he did.

"Insofar as Robbie goes," she continued, "I have no idea how *that's* going to work out. It would be nice if you could keep him while I'm with Liza. He gets off the bus as 2:45. Do you think you could keep yourself sober enough to watch your son while I'm here with Liza?"

Byron told her he could, in fact, keep himself sober enough to watch his own son.

"We'll see," she said. "The first time that I hear that you've been drinking around him, it will be the last time, I assure you. Now, I'm leaving. Get out of my way."

Byron moved back from the car as Samantha put it in reverse and squalled the tires pulling out of the parking space. She nearly ran over Byron's left foot, but he didn't seem to notice. She sped away into the twilight, her taillights flashing once at the intersection, and then she was gone. Byron stood like a statue. All emotion had seemed to drain from his body and soul. He felt perfectly empty inside. He felt so light that a strong puff of wind could pick him up and blow him away.

He had no idea how long he had been standing there when he felt a warm, soft hand on his neck. He looked to the right and there stood Amber, her eyes glistening in the light of the parking lot halogen bulbs.

She stood looking up at him for several silent moments. When she spoke, her voice was barely above a whisper. "I heard everything, Byron. I wasn't eavesdropping; I was just standing over by the door getting some air. She had no right to do that. Can't she see you are hurting, too? Can't she *see* that?"

Byron placed his hand over Amber's. "Samantha sees what Samantha sees," he said. "I don't factor into that. It's just the way it is. I actually owe her for slapping me just now. Until she did that, I honestly thought that part of me still loved her."

"And now?"

Byron smiled one of the grimmest smiles Amber had ever seen on a human face. "Now? Now, I can't even remember loving her in the first place. That happened to a different man." He shook himself. "I've got to go to the house, Amber. I've got to try to find something that is at least quasi-clean to change into. Otherwise, Rutherford might be able to run me out of here on hygienic grounds." He laughed bitterly, and turned to his truck. Amber stopped him. When he turned back, she was looking steadily at him in the harsh light.

"Go home and get your clothes. Take them to my place. I get off work in about an hour. I switched with Melissa Fry today. I don't even know why I did it. It just seemed like I needed tonight off. Take your clothes to the house. If you beat me there, the key is under that garden gnome you always made fun of. Drop your clothes by the washer and go take a shower. I'll be there soon."

"Amber," he said slowly, "I love you dearly. You know that. But I really can't deal with anything like this right now. I'm a mess, and the last thing I need is to add a romantic entanglement on top of everything else. I really do love you, kiddo. You have always been there for me. But it isn't fair to you, and to be honest, I'm not even sure if I could... *perform*...in that capacity right now." If someone had told Byron Williamson that he was even capable of blushing at this stage in his life, he would have laughed them right out of the room. It turned out that he was quite capable, after all.

Amber gave him one of the sexiest smiles he thought he had ever seen.

She said, "Well, Byron, you seem to have an awfully big opinion of your sexual appeal there, big boy. Not to offend or anything, but you sort of, well... you smell, Byron. Not the sexiest thing going." She turned serious. "Look, I'm not going for a roll in the hay here. After everything is settled, we may want to revisit this conversation. But right now, all I see in front of me is a friend that is in dire need of a shower, some clean clothes, and a long nap. Let me be your friend, Byron. That's all I'm asking."

Byron was shocked to find himself near tears. *Christ*, he thought, *all I do is cry anymore*. To Amber, he said, "Thank you. So much. You really don't know how much this means to me. But I have first watch with Liza, so I have to get my gear and get back here as quick as I can. Maybe next time, okay?"

Amber smiled again. "I just checked with the charge nurse in I.C.U. She told me to try to catch a hold of whichever one of you was going to stay tonight and tell them that Liza will be out until tomorrow morning, at the earliest. She got her night meds, and she's sleeping soundly. In any case, you know that I live four minutes from here. I've given the I.C.U. bunch my pager number. I've seen how you drive; you'll turn those four minutes into about two. Now, no more of your patented Byron Williamson bullshit: your house, some clothes, toothbrush, razor, et cetera, then over to Amber Jennson's house for a bath, some food, and some sleep. Got that, big boy?"

Byron face felt odd. It took him a minute to realize he had just given his first genuine smile in months. "Yes, ma'am," he said meekly.

Chapter Twelve

Samantha pulled in the driveway of their (her, dammit, *her*) house and turned off the car. She sat behind the wheel and tried to get a grip on herself. Was she being unfair to Byron? Yes, most likely. Did she give a damn? Not one bit, thank you very much. *Am I being a bitch?* she wondered. *Yes, I am, and I don't care. Byron did this to us. He may not have meant to, but he did it. He put a time bomb in my womb. It would have been bad enough if I had miscarried, or something, but no, that's not good enough. I have to have a time bomb that's set to go off* after *I've had time to love it more than life. Thanks very much, Byron. Why couldn't you just have bought me a fucking dog?*

Samantha knew how terrible this was, she knew how unfair she was being, but she was incapable of stopping it. She had tried, she really had. But every time she looked into Liza's pain-contorted face, she had to actively restrain herself from finding Byron and ripping his eyes out with her nails. Again; unfair, but true.

Samantha had stopped even pretending that there was anything in her heart but hatred for Byron. She had maintained the façade for the sake of the kids, but now, even that seemed to be falling apart. She could barely stand to be in Liza's hospital room with him for more than a few minutes without wanting to scream.

Samantha lowered her head to the steering wheel and gave in to the weeping that she knew she had to get out her system before she went in to Robbie. It was like a summer squall, short and violent. When it was over, she sat back up and wiped her eyes with a Kleenex from her purse. It seemed like even weeping was becoming more of a habit than a reaction anymore.

She got out of the car and walked up the steps of the porch. She was getting ready to put the key in the lock when the door swung open, revealing Robbie. He looked pale and tired, dark circles under his eyes. *Don't forget he's hurting, too*, Samantha thought. She held her arms out to him and held him for a moment in the doorway.

When they parted, Robbie led her into the kitchen, where he and the babysitter had been making dinner. The babysitter was a neighbor; a widow in her 60's named Helena Cartwright. Helena smiled at Samantha and asked how Liza was doing. Samantha just shook her head, cutting her eyes toward Robbie. Helena nodded and went back to working the dough for the pizza that she and Robbie had been working on. Robbie, a methodical boy, had all the ingredients lined up in a row next to each other on the counter top. As Helena asked for each one, he slapped it into her hand like a nurse assisting a doctor during an operation. Samantha smiled at them.

She went down the hallway to the bathroom to shower and change her clothes. As she went, she looked at the pictures lining the wall. She had removed each of them that had her and Byron alone in it.

She had left up the ones that contained the entire family, not wanting to upset the kids any more than necessary. She also never told them that each picture of their parents had been burned, one at a time, over a fire in the outdoor barbeque pit.

Samantha walked into the bathroom and turned on the shower as hot as it would go, which wasn't very. Long ago, Byron had turned the water heater's thermostat down, fearing that the kids would accidentally burn themselves. Samantha had agreed at the time, thinking that it was a good idea. Now, however, she found herself hurling another silent stream of obscenities at him.

She lowered her head and tried to control the rage that ran like venom through her whole body. Was she actually pissed at him because he had shown concern for their children's *welfare?* No, not really. She wasn't angry at Byron for being a good father. She was furious at him for being a *better* father than he had any right being. She realized that thought made little sense, but again decided that she didn't care. She stepped into the lukewarm shower and let the water fall across her face.

One of her real problems with Byron had nothing to do with the children, nothing to do with Liza's leukemia, for that matter, at all. Since they had first started dating, she had realized something about Byron Williamson that was different than the other boys she had dated. With them, a simple look from her would have them giving her whatever she wanted. *She* decided the conversation topics. *She* decided what movies they watched, or where they ate. She had simply accepted this as part of life. She was beautiful, she was charming, and she was wanted. Boys just did whatever she commanded.

But with Byron it had been different, right from the beginning. It wasn't that he didn't pay attention to her, much the opposite. He was always surprising her with small gifts, flowers and the like, when she very least expected them. He always asked her what movie she would like to see, or where she would like to eat. But there was something different about the whole situation, something that she couldn't quite put her finger on.

After several months of dating, it struck her one night as they sat across from each other at a local pizzeria, discussing their hopes for the future. She suddenly realized that even though Byron was always concerned about her opinions, it was *he* that led the conversations. *He* was always the one with something interesting to say. It wasn't that he was overbearing; again, he was quite the opposite. When she spoke, she could tell that he was actually listening to her, not just waiting for his turn to talk again.

No, it wasn't that Byron was mean or thoughtless of her wants and needs. It was, simply put, that he was more intelligent than she was.

Far more intelligent.

This was something utterly foreign to her. She had always made A's and B's throughout school, graduating with a 3.9 GPA. Byron had kept a 3.5 GPA, so she had automatically assumed that he was like the other boys. Good-looking, attentive, and slightly less intelligent than she was.

She realized that night while eating pizza just how wrong she had been. Byron was *spooky* smart. He seemed to know what she was going to say, or what she wanted even before she did herself. One would think that a girl with a good-looking boy that seemed to dote on her *and* could anticipate her every whim would have been a godsend. Instead, it made her feel a little uncomfortable.

Over the course of the meal, she began asking questions of Byron that she had never asked any of her other boyfriends. What did he score on the ACT? Byron looked uncomfortable and tried to change the subject, but she persisted. He finally mumbled the number thirty-one, and then in a rush, said it was mostly luck.

She was flabbergasted. A 31 on the ACT?!? That was damn near perfect. She herself had scored a 25, and felt pretty damned proud of it. He could get into any college in America with a score like that. Why, then, did he keep a 3.5 GPA? If he could score a 31 on the ACT, he could have been valedictorian with no problem. Again, she could tell that this line of questioning was making Byron uncomfortable, but she pushed on. Why the lower GPA when he could have done so much better?

After several minutes of uncomfortable silence, Byron looked at Samantha with a slight frown on his face. When he spoke, his voice was low and devoid of emotion.

"Sammy, do you know what it's like to know that you are different? To know that if you acted the way you really could, did the things that you knew you were able to, that people would make a big deal out of it? I mean, you're a cheerleader, you're smart, and you are the most beautiful girl I have ever seen. People want to be near you because of that. But if I actually did what I *can* do, people wouldn't want to be near me. I'd be the freak that is too smart for his own good. My friends would stop hanging out with me, not that I have all that many. The teachers were fine with my performance in school right up to that damned ACT. I tried to get out of taking it. I told them I was sick that day, but they told me that it didn't matter, that I had plenty of opportunities to take it before graduation. So, if I showed up sick every time they gave the damn thing, somebody would have caught on."

He stopped talking for a moment, his eyes taking on a far-off cast. When he started speaking again, Samantha could tell that he was talking as much to himself as he was to her.

"So, I took the thing. I thought about throwing it, you know, just randomly answering the questions wrong. But something in me wouldn't allow it. My dad, I guess. He always told me, from the time I was a little boy, that if you choose to do something, do it right. I figured that a 3.5 GPA was all right, because I was doing well enough to satisfy everyone. But when they put that damned test in front of me, I just couldn't throw it. I felt like I *had* to do my best. Hell," he laughed, "I even tried to shave off a point or two here and there, just to keep my composite score a bit lower. I even fucked that up, apparently.

I probably got lucky when I put some random answers down, and they turned out to be right." He gave a rueful chuckle.

Samantha looked at Byron with open amazement.

"Do you mean to tell me that you tried to throw some of the answers on the ACT and *still* made a 31 on the damn thing?"

Byron was actively uncomfortable now, and tried to change the subject, but Samantha was having none of it. She had set her mind to getting to the bottom of this, and by-God, Philip Murphy's girl got to the bottom of something once she set her mind to it.

"Answer my question, Byron. Did you really try to do poorly on the ACT and still come out with a 31?"

He shook his head. "No, I didn't try to do *poorly*; I just didn't try to as good as I could have. Sammy, I'm just a normal guy. My friends are all normal. That's what I want to be: normal. Just that. It's just that things are so *easy* for me. I don't bother studying for a test, I just scan my notes right before I take it. I'm not bragging, I swear. That's just the way I am. I can't help it. When you start to do things like score really high on a test like the ACT, people look at you differently. I just don't want anyone to look at me differently, that's all. Please, keep this to yourself. I love you, and if you love me too, please don't let anyone one know about that stupid damn test, okay?"

The raw need in his eyes convinced her. "I won't tell anyone, Byron. But what about the teachers and the counselors? They've got copies of the test, and surely they know what you made on it."

Byron set his jaw. "Yeah, they know. They wanted to make a big deal out of it, but I told them that if they tried, I would tell everyone I cheated on it."

Samantha gasped. "You can't do that! You could get into serious trouble!"

Byron smiled. "Calm down, Sammy. Turns out it was an empty threat, because the room was under video surveillance, and they knew that I hadn't cheated. Don't you just love modern technology? I don't think that watching someone on video is ethically right, but what do I know? But I think that me *saying* that I would was enough to convince them to keep a lid on it." He blew out a breath. "I just want to finish up this last semester and go on into the Army. I've already talked to the recruiter, and took the Army's version of the ACT. It's called the ASVAB. I'm in just as soon as we graduate."

Samantha rolled her eyes. "Let me guess, you did quite well on the Army test, too, right?"

Byron grinned again. "Well, let's just say I did well enough to pretty much get my pick of what MOS I go into."

"What's a MOS?"

"It's the Army's version of a job specialty. You get to pick what sort of job you want to do if you score high enough on the test."

She smiled at him. "So what, you're going to be a five-star general, right? Or maybe the head of NATO or something?"

He laughed. "Nope, nothing quite so dramatic for this old boy. I'm going to be a medic. They wanted me to do some college first and go to OCS, but I turned them down. I've thought about it, and I think that's what I want to do. Once I get out, I can get on as a paramedic, and go to school in my spare time. I was thinking about being a P.A."

"Okay, you're starting to piss me off with all the abbreviations here, buddy boy. ASVAB, MOS, OCS, P.A. Enough, already. What's a P.A.?"

He laughed. "ASVAB is Armed Services Vocational Aptitude Battery. OCS is Officer's Candidate School. MOS is Military Occupational Specialties. I don't plan on being in long enough to be an officer. If I was going to make it my career, I might have, I guess. A P.A. is a Physician's Assistant. You know Tommy Granger that works at Dawkins Methodist hospital?"

She nodded. "Yeah, he's like, ten years older than us or something, right?"

"Well, closer to five, but yeah, he graduated a while back. He's a P.A. They make great money, and the hours are pretty cool. I can work three 12-hour shifts a week and still go to school"

"Okay, judging by the job title, I suppose a P.A. assists a doctor, but by doing what?"

"Just anything that needs to be done. Setting bones, suturing wounds, things like that. They're a lot like a doctor, but they can't do surgery or prescribe narcotics and stuff like that."

She looked at him for several moments. Finally she said, "Okay, I get it. You're really smart. I can handle that. I even kind of like it, although it's going to take some getting used to. But I really need to know one thing, okay?"

Byron looked at her dead-on. "Ask away."

"You could get a scholarship to anywhere with your grades and that ACT score. You told my dad you were going to go to college on the G.I. Bill once you got out. You don't need a G.I. Bill. With your grades and test scores, you could get pretty much a free ride to anywhere you wanted to go. So, why are you joining the Army? Do you realize that everything between us will have to go on the back burner for a few years while you do that? Have you thought about that?"

Byron sat looking down at his half-eaten piece of pizza. Then he looked back into Samantha's eyes.

"Yeah, Sammy, it *will* put us on the back burner. But what I told your dad was the flat truth. I want to serve my country. My dad served in Vietnam. My uncle served In Korea, and both of my grandfathers served in World War Two. What happened on September

11th hasn't gone away. There are still bad people out there, Sammy. They need to be caught. I feel like I have a duty to serve, that's all. I can't explain it better than that." He shrugged his shoulders helplessly. "If you don't think you can wait for me, I understand."

"It's not that I don't understand," she said. "It's just that I don't want you to forget your duty to *me*."

Byron reached across the table and took her hand. His voice was the most serious she had ever heard it. "I will *never* forget that, Sammy. *Never*."

Samantha opened her eyes in the shower. *Never*, she thought. *Right. Your duty to me ended the moment Liza became sick, you son of a bitch.*

She stepped out of the shower and dried herself off. She went back to the kitchen, where Helena and Robbie were pulling the pizza out of the oven with a flourish. Robbie's smile should have warmed her heart. Instead, she felt ice form around it.

Never…right. Fuck never, Byron. Never is here and now.

Chapter Thirteen

Amber Jennson's house looked like something out of a Brothers Grimm fairy tale. It was small, but everything was in its place, and everything was immaculate. *How in the hell does she have the time to keep everything so clean*, Byron thought, *with the hours that she works?* Then he realized that she lived alone, had no pets, no children, and no husband to be making messes that needed to be cleaned up in the first place. Still, he was impressed with the tidy little home.

He dropped the garbage bag of his dirty clothes by the washer, meaning to run them through once he had taken a shower. He stepped into her bathroom and was overwhelmed by the various fragrances that hit his olfactory senses. The smells weren't cloying, far from it. They all seemed to complement each other subtly, with the overall effect of a whispered *a woman lives here.* He let the scents soothe him for a moment, and then stripped out of his grungy clothing. To his utter embarrassment, there were skid marks in his underwear. He silently vowed to have *those* bad boys safely ensconced in the washing machine long before Amber made her appearance on the scene.

He stepped into the shower and turned the water on as hot as he could stand it. He stood there under the needle spray until his muscles began to relax. He breathed deeply of the steamy air, and began to think it was possible that he might pass for human again at some point soon. He slid down the shower wall and sat on the little bench built into it. The combination of hot water and exhaustion had the expected effect: he was soon fast asleep.

He woke to the sound of Amber singing along with an old Etta James song in the kitchen. With a guilty start, he jerked into a standing position and turned off the water, which had now grown tepid. He opened the shower door. *Oh, Christ,* he thought. His clothes were gone. Had she seen his filthy underwear? Of course she had. *Damn.* He looked around with mounting panic as he realized there were no towels to be had. With a sigh, he closed his eyes and yelled into the kitchen.

"Amber? Uh…I have a slight problem here."

He heard her laugh. A few moments later, the bathroom door began to open. Byron, having no other recourse, shut the shower door again. The glass of the door was marbled, but it was more for show than anything else. He could see her quite clearly, which meant she could see him just as clearly.

"What seems to be the problem, big boy?" she asked, laughter audible in her voice.

"I think you know damn well what the problem is," he growled. "Why the hell aren't there any towels in here?"

"Well," she said, "I usually have sense enough to bring my towel with me if I'm going to take a shower, sweetie."

"Ha-frigging-ha ha. Very funny, dear heart. Well, since I obviously didn't have sense enough to do that, could you possibly get me one?"

"Well," she said, "I'm not sure if there are any clean. Tomorrow's my laundry day, you see. I might be able to find you a washcloth, would that help?"

Byron growled. "Amber…"

She laughed again, a high, sweet sound. "Hold on, you big baby, I'll go get you one. Jeez, *men*…"

Amber went into the hallway and returned with a large terrycloth towel. She held it out, just shy of Byron's outstretched hands. "C'mon, big guy, you can do it!"

"When I get out of here, and am fully clothed, I am going to make you pay for this, Amber Jennson. You will pay dearly."

"Oooh," she said, "I am *so* frightened. Whatever shall I do?"

Byron finally succeeded in snatching the towel from Amber, who gave him an unabashed look from head to toe. Once her eyes returned to his she said, "Nice. Very nice, indeed.'

"You'll think nice!" He shouted and made as if to grab her. She laughed and pranced out into the hallway. With a mischievous glint in her eye, she said, "Do you think you might be able to hold off on the 'making me pay dearly' part of the evening for just a bit? I've got something on the stove that will probably taste much better if it isn't scorched." With that, she walked down the hallway and into the kitchen.

Byron stood dripping water, a towel draped loosely around his waist. Was this what he had been missing for so long? The simple things, like a home-cooked meal and laughing with another human being? *Jesus*, he said to himself, *I've really let myself go to hell.*

To his horror, Amber had already washed all of his clothes and had them in the dryer. As he walked in, she said, "Hey, big guy, I just went ahead and threw everything in to wash. If you had clean clothes in there with the dirty ones, I've got to tell you, I couldn't tell the difference."

"Well, it's not that I'm not grateful," he said, "But what am I supposed to wear until they get dry? I'm not really all that keen on sitting around in a bath towel for the next hour or so."

She smiled. "I think that the towel suits you just fine, but if you're going to be such a prude about things, go into my bedroom and open the bottom drawer of my dresser. There are about a million sets of hospital scrubs in there, and there will probably be at least one pair that should fit you."

Byron did as she told him, and managed to find a set of scrub bottoms that were only about two sizes too small. The tops were impossible. If he tried to wear one of those, he would look like the Incredible Hulk the first time he reached for something, ripping every seam on it. He yelled back into the kitchen and asked her if she maybe had an old tee shirt he could borrow.

"Yeah, I actually think I do," she replied. "My brother was here a year or so ago painting my hutch and he had on an old Mark Chestnut tee shirt that got paint all over it. I told him I'd wash it, but he never got it back. Will that work?"

Byron laughed. "I'll think of something," he said, half to himself.

"What?"

"I said that'll be something. I'm sure it'll be just fine." It was. It was a little tight through the chest, but then again, Byron had lost a fair amount of weight over the last several months, so it wasn't so tight as to be a problem.

He walked back into the kitchen to the smell of vegetable lasagna and garlic bread. Amber had opened a bottle of white wine and poured them both a glass. He walked over to the table and said, "Really Amber, this is too much. I could have helped, or something. You're not my maid. I feel like a total jerk, just showing up here with a bag of filthy clothes and you washing them and feeding me. I don't know how I let you talk me into this."

"I talked you into this because this is exactly what you need, and you know it. You just need a good meal, something clean to put on, and a good night's sleep. Once you've had all three of those things, all will begin to look right in the world."

He grinned at her. "Well, I sure as hell hope so. I know that my stomach is reasonably sure my throat has been cut. Let's eat, and then *I* do the dishes."

They spent the remainder of the meal in companionable silence, the scratching of silverware on plates the loudest noise made. For the first time in a very long time, Byron had a glass of wine that he drank for the taste, not just so it would get him from standing to the fetal position as rapidly as possible. When the meal was over, he leaned back in his chair, looking dreamily off into space.

"You know what?" he asked. "I think that very well may have been the first home-cooked meal I've eaten in… months. I mean that. Literally months. Mostly I eat at whatever burger joint we're close enough to between runs. And at home… well, I don't think you could safely classify anything I make a "home-cooked meal". Maybe a "home-scorched inedible pile of waste". That was great Amber. I mean that, that was really great. I don't think I've felt this good in forever. Thank you so much for having me."

She smiled back at him. "You big goof, you could have been eating like this the whole time if you weren't such a dumb ass. I generally cook at least once a day, you know." She saw the uncomfortable look on his face and rushed forward. "Look, Byron, I know how things have been between you and Samantha. Okay? I'm not blind. I also know that half of the hospital will be telling the other half that you spent the night here tonight. It's a small town, right? The point is, I don't give a damn what they think, or what they say. You and I have known each other since we were kids, and if it offends the Women's Auxiliary that you and I spent the night under the same roof, well, then the hell with them!"

Byron sat looking at her with a lop-sided grin. "Quite the little hell-fire when you get riled, aren't you?"

"Big boy, you don't know the half of it. Now, help me with these dishes. No free rides here, bub."

They spent the rest of the evening watching meaningless sitcoms on television and talking about the old days. Byron called the hospital three different times and received the exact same answer to each call. Liza was asleep, and was most likely going to stay that way until the morning. If anything changed, he'd get the call. Byron thanked them each time and then hung up.

Finally, around midnight, Amber flipped the television off and stood up. She walked over to where Byron sat on the recliner and offered him her hand. He took it, a confused look on his face. She blew out and exasperated breath and said, "I'm tired, Byron. I'm ready for bed. Aren't you tired?"

He was, and said so. But as they began to walk towards Amber's bedroom, he began to get nervous. He stammered a few times, trying to figure out just how to say it so Amber wouldn't be hurt. She took the ball and ran with it, however, saving him from having to embarrass himself.

"Byron, honey, you know I love you. I always have. And to be perfectly honest, the thought of you in my bed makes me just a wee bit shaky in the knees. If this were some other night, I promise you, I would take you to that bed and fuck you like I was paying for it. Tonight, however, I think I'd just like it if we held onto one another and went to sleep. What do you say?"

The intentional crudity had shocked him into a laugh, and he lost all his nervousness. "Okay, kiddo. Let's get some sleep. I've got to be up early to get back to Sacred anyway. I want to be there when Liza wakes up."

They climbed into bed and formed a perfect spoon, as if they had been sleeping that way their whole lives. Amber was on the threshold of sleep when she heard Byron say her name.

"Hmmm?"

"Did you really threaten to fuck me like you were paying for it?"

She snorted laughter and hit him with a pillow. "Go to sleep, you idiot," she said.

Five minutes later, the only sound in the bedroom was that of their breathing.

It was perfectly in sync.

Chapter Fourteen

Byron was at Sacred Hearts by six the next morning, and was told by the nurse at the main desk that Liza had slept all night, without any trouble. He got himself a coffee from the cafeteria and went into Liza's room. She lay surrounded by her stuffed animals, just as she had been the night before. To Byron it didn't appear that she had moved at all. He ran his hand through her baby-fine hair and kissed her on the forehead. He sat in one of the high-backed chairs in the room and drank his coffee. He half hoped that Liza would wake up soon, so they could have some time together before Samantha got there. He knew that it would be better for Liza if she slept, but he couldn't help hoping that she might awaken so they could have some Liza-Daddy time. It was something he had gotten precious little of lately, and he missed it like mad.

By seven-thirty, he had resigned himself to the fact that Samantha would be there before Liza woke. He was working on a plan to get Samantha to go back on her statement of the last night and let him stay a bit longer, at least until Liza woke, when he heard her say his name.

"Daddy?"

Byron's face lit up. "Hey there, baby! How's my little girl doing today?"

"I hurting all over, Daddy. Like when Robbie falled off his bike."

Tears stung the corner of Byron's eyes; the treacherous bastards were always so close anymore. He slammed them back viciously. When he spoke, he was amazed at how normal his voice sounded.

"I know, baby. Robbie hurt all over when he fell off his bike that day. But, he was fine the next day, right?"

Liza looked out her window and sighed. Her voice was so soft that Byron had to lean in close to hear it.

"Yeah, he was okay on the next day. But I not falled off a bike. I hurting all over *all the time*. Why come I hurting all the time if I not falled anywhere, Daddy?"

Byron could no longer stem the tears. They fell, unheeded, into his lap. He stroked Liza's hair, over and over.

"I don't know why you have to hurt all the time, baby. Daddy would do anything in the world to make it stop. I promise you I would."

"Why's you cryin', Daddy? Did you falled?"

Byron wept openly now. He tried to stop. He didn't want Liza to become afraid, to add to her pain and confusion. Because he could think of nothing else, he simply told her the truth,

"Baby, Daddy is crying because you hurt. When you hurt, it makes Daddy's heart hurt, too. It's not your fault that Daddy's heart hurts, just like it's not your fault that you hurt. It's just that sometimes, even Daddies have to cry. Because they love their babies so much. Do you understand?"

Liza smiled so sweetly at Byron that he literally thought his heart would rupture in his chest. He felt a wave a rage so powerful that it gave him tunnel vision for a moment. If it was God's will that his baby girl die a little at a time, then Byron longed for the day when he finally met Him. If he could, he would knock God flat on his ass.

And then kick his fucking teeth out.

Liza's smile faltered for a moment. *Oh shit, she saw that in my eyes*, he thought. *Got to get a grip here.* He smiled at her. "Are you hungry?" he asked brightly. "You want me to go get you something to eat?"

"No. I's not hungry now. I's just tired. 'Sides, it's not time for brefus yet. The girls told me."

"Well, Daddy says it's time for brefus any time Liza's ready for it, and Daddy is in charge." What Liza had said played back in his head. "What girls told you it wasn't time for breakfast yet, honey?"

Liza pointed to his right.

"Them. They's my new-best friends. They's gonna take me to Heaven soon, and I won't be hurtin' no more. That'll be nice. No more hurtin' for Liza." This last she almost sang.

Byron looked to his right and slapped his hands to his mouth. He shoved them together just as hard as he could. If he hadn't, his screams would have probably scared Liza to death.

"Was a matter, Daddy? Why's you holdin' you mouth like that?" she said.

Standing next to Byron, so close that he could almost touch them, were three little girls, all around four or five years old. In unison, they turned from Liza and looked at Byron. They simply looked at him for a moment, and then returned their dark eyes to Liza.

Byron stood on legs he could not feel. He shambled to Liza's bed and took her hands in his own. He leaned down until their foreheads were touching. Whispering to her, he said, "Liza, baby, I want you to listen to me. This is very important. Those girls may be your new best friends, but you are not to go *anywhere* with them, do you understand me? Not anywhere *at all*. You stay right here until Daddy gets back. Do you promise me?"

Liza's eyes had grown huge in her confusion and fear. "I promise, Daddy. But they's my new-best friends. They's gonna take me to Heaven. Don't you wan' me to go to Heaven, Daddy? Go to Heaven an' no be hurtin' no more?"

"Oh Liza, baby, of *course* Daddy wants you to go to Heaven! And you will, too. Just not right now. You may have to hurt a bit longer, but you have to stay here in this bed. You do *not* follow those little girls anywhere. Remember, you promised. Daddy will explain later, all right?"

Liza looked doubtful, but agreed. "Ho-kay, Daddy. Liza won't go anywheres with my new-best friends until Daddy says I can."

Byron leaned over and kissed Liza on that softest of spots, just between her eyes. His tears continued to fall, and one landed on Liza's cheek. She giggled. "That tickles, Daddy!"

"I know, sweetheart. That's what Daddy's do. We tickle our babies."

He turned and looked at the children standing at the foot of the bed. If he could, he would have forced them from the room, but he knew that there was no way that could happen. They were not there *for* him; they were there *because* of him.

And now he had to take care of that.

<u>Chapter Fifteen</u>

Samantha arrived at promptly eight o'clock. She seemed surprised that Byron was adhering so stringently to the laws she had laid down on the previous evening. No more was she in Liza's room than Byron kissed his little girl and left without a backward look. Samantha felt almost put-out by this, but realizing that he was simply following her directions to the letter, she relented. Maybe if he had followed her orders this closely when they had been married, they might still *be* married. That thought was another of her little "bitch bubbles" that surfaced whenever she was around Byron for more than a few seconds. She shut it out of her mind and turned to Liza.

Byron didn't even give Samantha a passing glance as he left the room. His path was clear to him now. As he rushed down the hallway, a four-word refrain beat across his mind like a drum. *Sins of the father, sins of the father, sins of the father, sins of the father.* Although he was unaware of it, this refrain was in perfect time with the beating of his heart.

Byron's mouth was dry. When he exhaled, he could taste diesel fumes and sand. It was a taste he had not encountered for a very long time. He clamped his eyes shut and stopped in the middle of the hallway. The cords stuck out in his neck, and a large vein throbbed in center of his forehead. Had a doctor been passing that way at that moment, he would have almost certainly pegged Byron as someone suffering from an acute case of hypertension at the very least, and more likely a heart attack. Fortunately for Byron, he had the I.C.U. hallway to himself for the moment.

Byron opened his eyes and began moving. He was almost at a run when he realized that if he allowed himself to start running, he would lose the last vestiges of control he had, and turn himself over completely to the panic that had been fluttering around his mind like so many barn swallows since Liza's introduction of her new friends.

He rounded the last corner of the I.C.U. hallway and headed for the elevator. He hated the things, and almost invariably took the stairs, but today his mind was a thousand miles away. Had he been required to crawl through a sewer pipe full of snakes to reach his destination, we would have done so with the exact same vacant expression on his face.

Once in the elevator, he hit the button for the ground floor and stood waiting for the doors to close. He heard someone yelling to hold the door, and he instinctively reached out to do just that. *How odd is that*, he thought, *my world is coming apart around me, and I'm still instinctively polite. Mom would have been proud.* This struck him hilarious, and he suddenly found himself laughing. He did not care for the strained, frightened sound coming out of his mouth one bit.

Heaving his two hundred and eighty pound bulk into the elevator with Byron was Father Daniel Bern, Sacred Hearts' resident priest. As he caught his breath, he looked Byron over. When he could speak, he did so in his flat, declarative style.

"Byron, I've been hearing some very disturbing things concerning you. Things that I think need to be addressed, and right soon. Wouldn't you agree?"

Byron opened his mouth to give his standard answer, the one that explained all his woes away with simple exhaustion and family discord. Instead, he found himself reaching out and hitting the Stop button on the elevator control panel. He turned to the priest.

"Okay, Father. Where would you like to begin?"

Father Bern was taken slightly aback. He had known Byron for several years, and had expected nothing short of resistance from him about this. At the very least, he expected Byron to tell him there was nothing wrong with him. At the very worst, Bern feared that Byron might follow that statement up with a left hook. Bern had heard Doctor Rutherford's side of the story about the altercation outside Liza's E.R. room. Rutherford had always struck Bern as a bit of a pompous windbag, but in conjunction with all the other stories circulating about Byron's behavior of late, he was forced to concede to the possibility that Byron had actually attacked the doctor, although Bern seriously doubted that it had been anything as dramatic as Rutherford had made out.

Still, although he was caught off guard by Byron's willingness to discuss his problems, Bern had been a Catholic priest for over four decades, and was equipped to handle this sudden change of heart with aplomb. He smiled at Byron and said simply, "Well, son, I think we should start at the beginning. That always worked best for me."

Byron thought it over for a moment and then said, "No, not the beginning. I think we need to start in the middle. Otherwise, none of this will make any sense." He laughed. "Like it will make sense, anyway, no matter how I tell it."

Bern nodded as if this were the most normal thing in the world. "Byron, I really want to hear this, and I really want to help you, but I think that maybe the elevator may not be the best place to have this conversation. What do you say we adjourn to my office?"

"No," Byron said, "Not your office. I want to go to the chapel, if that's all right. It's quiet. I could use a little quiet. Is that all right?"

"Of course it is," Bern said. "I think the chapel is a great idea. Lead the way, son."

Byron restarted the elevator, and they got off on the second floor. They walked down the hallway, their heels clicking on the tile floor. Neither said anything on the way to the chapel, each in his own thoughts. Bern was thinking of the best way to pull as much pain out of Byron as possible, to bring it into the light and thereby dissipate it. Byron was thinking of nothing at all, his mind a low hum of background noise.

They entered the chapel, the light diffusing through the stained glass windows creating a cool, dim sanctuary. Without discussing it, they both made their way to the front of the chapel and took a seat on the first pew. Father Bern turned towards Byron, his left leg over his right, his hands clasped gently and resting on his left knee. He secretly thought of this as his "Give it to me" pose. With his head cocked slightly to one side, he gave off the impression of patience and understanding incarnate.

Byron simply sat, his head down and his hands dangling loosely between his knees. After a few moments, he turned to look at Father Bern.

"You know I was in Iraq, right?"

Bern nodded. "Of course, son. All Sacred Hearts employee files make it across my desk sooner or later. You didn't hear that from me, by the way. We would never breach confidentiality, you know."

Byron nodded. "Yeah, I guess it would make sense for you have some background info on any of us that might wander your way, seeking a little spiritual guidance. Forewarned is forearmed, right?"

Bern flapped a hand in a "you know how it is" sort of way. "It does help me do my job somewhat if I understand some of the underlying problems an employee might be facing."

Byron gave Bern a smirk. "And I'll bet that *my* file has occupied a pretty large part of your desk lately, hasn't it?"

"Son, I'm not going to lock horns with you. Yes, I've been reading your file. And I think you and I both know why. There's been a lot going on in your life, Ram. Things that would take a lesser man to pieces."

Byron grinned at the older man. "Two things, Father. One, that's the first time you've ever called me Ram, and two, I appreciate the fact that you don't consider me a 'lesser man'".

Bern laughed. "No, son, I don't think of you as a lesser man. I think you're a fine one, and one that's worth keeping on the right track. Just out of curiosity, why *do* they call you 'Ram', anyway?"

Byron grinned. "Once, about two years ago, we were dispatched on a multiple vehicle crash at the intersection just before you get to Sacred. I mean, you could *see* the wreck from the hospital. We made it on scene without any problems, and most of the patients were all right, just cuts and bruises. There was this one kid, though, maybe fifteen years old. He had a laceration that ran from his hairline down to his collarbone. He was messing with his seat belt, and had taken the shoulder harness off and put it behind his back, the way kids do. When the wreck happened, he was thrown forward and into the dashboard. The glove box had pooped open, and there was a ruler, of all things, in it. The kid hit the ruler somehow. It missed his carotid artery by about half a centimeter. Even so, this kid was bleeding badly. I mean, he was gouting blood everywhere."

"'Gouting, son'? What, exactly, does 'gouting' mean?" asked Bern.

"Ah, it's just one of those things you pick up. I've said that since I was a kid. Like pusgetti instead of spaghetti, you know? Anyway, this kid was losing blood fast. I had a line in, and we were only about a hundred yards from the hospital, you know? I figured we could get his volume up in the E.R. Well, the lookie-loos decided they hadn't seen enough blood on the pavement yet, and they were all standing around gawking. Got out of their cars and shit to see better. People are weird, you know?"

"Yes, as a matter of fact, I am aware of that fact."

"Anyway, the local P.D. hadn't made it on scene yet. Nothing against them, you know. Like I said, we were within a stone's throw of the wreck, so of course we got there first. Well, we're all loaded up, I've got this kid in the back and he's bleeding hell-to-breakfast all over me. I yell up at my partner to hurry up and get us to the E.R. He hollers back that he can't, because all these idiots had the road blocked with their cars. Some of them were out taking pictures with their cell phones, if you can believe *that*. Man, that pissed me off, *bad*. I grabbed the P.A. and keyed it up as loud as it would go and screamed into it that anyone that didn't want their vehicles rammed out of the way, they had best fucking move them. I guess that worked, because a few seconds later, we started moving. We got that kid into the E.R. and got him squared away. Some of the guys thought it would be funny to get one of those ram hood ornaments off an old Dodge Ram truck and superglue it to my locker. After that, the name just sort of stuck."

"I see," Bern said. "And had those people not moved, would you have rammed their vehicles?"

"Damn right I would have. I would have smashed the hell out of the most expensive one that I could find in the way and then *dared* the owner to try and sue."

Bern looked at Byron for a moment. "You know," he finally said, "You are really a quite remarkable person."

Byron shook his head. "Yeah, all I'm missing is a cape and a kick-ass ride and I'm a superhero. Anyway, so you know about Iraq, then. What I'm about to tell you I guarantee you haven't read in my file, because it isn't *in* my file. Not my personnel file from Sacred, anyway. You could possibly get it from the Army, but they don't much care to have their dirty laundry aired in public, so if you try, be prepared for a mountain of bullshit."

Byron grimaced, and began to rub his hands together, back and forth. The soft whisper of his calloused hands was the loudest thing in the chapel. Bern waited patiently. Finally, Byron began to speak.

"We were in a convoy, heading for Fallujah. It was no biggie, nothing we hadn't done a thousand times. There were five of us in the Humvee that day, but the only one that really matters in Henderson. And God, Henderson was starting…"

Chapter Sixteen

Henderson was starting to get on Byron's nerves. The monotonous "The fuck you lookin' at? Huh? The fuck you lookin' at, you haji bitches?" was really getting old. It was hot, it was uncomfortable, and it stank. Beyond that, now he had to listen to Henderson's unending stream of bullshit. He reached up and tugged on Henderson's ACU leg to get his attention. Henderson looked down from the turret, his eyes full of rage. "The fuck do *you* want, Williamson?"

"I want to know why the hell you're acting like a fucking desk-jockey on his first convoy, that's what. Those people aren't doing a damn thing to you. You see a sniper? One of them got a RPG? Is Saddam hiding behind one of those kids? What? They're just standing there, man. Chill your shit."

Henderson gave Byron a contemptuous look. "You wouldn't know the difference between a sniper and a fucking short-order cook. You're the medic. So why don't you shut the fuck up until somebody needs a Tylenol?"

Byron wasn't one to pull rank, but he *did* outrank the little fuck, and he wasn't going to put up with this shit. "Hey, *Private* Henderson, do you have a problem? If you do, we could use this little break to step outside the vehicle and remedy it."

Henderson actually began lowering himself from the turret and for a moment Byron thought he was going to be able to off-load some of his frustration and anger onto this little piss ant by stomping the hell out of him. Before things could progress to that state, however, First Sergeant Fleming's gravelly voice cut through the interior of the Humvee like a thunder god.

"You leave that gun position without permission Henderson, and I will personally see to it you spend the rest of your time in sunny Iraq digging latrines. I shit you not, soldier. Now, take your fucking post." He turned his head to look at Byron. "And you, Sergeant Williamson, why exactly are you letting that little fuck-ball get to you? Here I've been, giving you credit for having better sense."

Byron smiled abashedly back at his First Sergeant. "Sorry, Sarge. I forgot to take my Midol today. Just got hot and bothered, is all. Momentary lapse of judgment. Won't happen again."

"Good. Now, where the fuck is our lead gun truck? They were just supposed to scout to the first intersection." He keyed up the mike and called out to the lead unit. There was nothing but static. He repeated the call. More static. Fleming began to look a little worried as he called out to the unit again. Before he could finish his interrogative, the world seemed to rip itself apart around them.

"Contact left!" someone screamed over the com. This was followed instantly with someone else screaming "Contact right!" Rounds began zipping down the length of the convoy, high-pitched whines that sometimes smacked into one of the vehicles with a *bonk!* The gun trucks opened up, their heavy automatic weapons blasting large holes in the concrete buildings in front of and to the sides of the convoy. In the turret of Byron's Humvee, Henderson was screaming "Gimme a fucking target! Gimme a *target!*"

The incoming fire had already begun to taper off. This was just another ambush, set up by lightly armed Iraqis that were already thinking about where they were going to run, and how fast they could get there. The amount of out-going fire began to dwindle, as well, as the gunners realized that their targets were getting the hell out of Dodge. Up in his turret, however, Henderson was still screaming about wanting a target. Finally, he stopped screaming. In the next few seconds, all was still, and everyone in the Humvee heard him say in a conversational voice, "Fuck it. I'll *make* a target."

Henderson swiveled the .50 caliber automatic rifle around and began to hammer into the group of Iraqi civilians that had been standing on the corner. They had, in the course of the firefight, most sensibly dropped to the ground. As the large .50 caliber rounds began slamming into the ground around them, they dropped again, trying madly to find some cover, *any* cover. All but three. Three Iraqi girls; all dressed alike and looking like sisters, finally gave in to their panic. They jumped up and fled back towards the buildings behind them. Drawn by their movement, Henderson shifted his fire to them. Before the horrified eyes of the men in the Humvee, the little girls' bodies seemed to disintegrate. Blood hung in a haze in the dusty air. The children fell like wheat. A stream of blood from one of them spurted into the air and seemed to hang there like rubies for a moment before it splashed back to earth.

Byron didn't think. He gave absolutely no thought whatsoever to his next action. He turned his rifle, slid it up under the Kevlar body armor Henderson was wearing, and fired it four times. The rounds tore up through Henderson's body, ripping his left shoulder off. One of the rounds exited his armor at the neck and entered his face, just behind his left mandible. He dropped straight down like a reverse Jack-in-the-box and lay twitching on the Humvee floor, which quickly began filling with his blood. Byron jerked his weapon free from Henderson's still-twitching body.

Byron ripped open his door and was running towards the fallen civilians before he even realized that he was moving. He could hear Fleming screaming in the background, but tunnel vision had set in, and he could only see the bleeding Iraqis. As he slid to a stop among them, he was already doing a subconscious triage. Miraculously, not one of the civilians that had dropped back to earth when Henderson had begun firing was directly hit. Several had long scrapes, oozing blood. These Byron figured were from chips of concrete that had been thrown up from the high-caliber shells. All of them were screaming. Absently, Byron set these wounds aside for later treatment.

He crawled forward on his hands and knees toward the place the girls had been shot. Before he even got close, his logical mind knew there was nothing to be done. The huge rounds had done their work well. There was little left of the children that was recognizable. However, Byron was no longer running on logic. He began picking up the pieces and trying to reassemble them. He was trying to fit one of the girl's arms back into place when First Sergeant Fleming approached him, very slowly.

"Sergeant Williamson, I need you to place your weapon on the ground and step away from it. Do this now." Fleming's voice was calm, as if he were asking Byron to pass him the salt.

Byron looked at Fleming curiously, not tracking him at all. "What?" he asked his voice dazed and dull.

"Your weapon, Sergeant. I need you to place it on the ground. Can you do that for me, Byron?"

Byron looked at his rifle. He had it leaning against him secured by a bungee strap while he worked on the children. He unhooked the carabineer from the strap with one hand and handed the rifle off to Fleming, never noticing how tight the First Sergeant's finger had become on the trigger of his own weapon. "Here," Byron said. "I don't need it. I need some gauze, though, and some tape. Oh, and I'll need some sterile bandages. Some splints, too. How much plasma do we have on hand? And QuikClot, I need as much of that as we've got."

Fleming shouldered Byron's rifle, ignoring Byron's increasingly fast-paced babbling. He looked around at the men that had gathered helplessly. *This* shit was most definitely *not* covered in the manual. In the space of just a few hellish seconds, he had seen one of his men intentionally gun down civilian children, and then watched *another* of his men blow the first one's guts out. Now that man was crawling through the remains of three little girls, trying to put them back together like some sort of fucking Erector Set. Fleming looked around for help, but the Convoy Commander was busy making sure that the flanks were secure.

He turned and found one of the soldiers on the LZ team standing there, looking like he was about to vomit. Fleming grabbed him by the shoulder and said, "I want a bird in the air, *right now*. Set up an LZ beyond the rear of the convoy. Tell them we've got..." What the hell *did* they have? "Tell them we've got one American KIA, and several civilian wounded, and three civilian dead. Tell them we also need... just tell them that the convoy medic will be being evacuated, too." That Byron was going to be on that Blackhawk, Fleming knew beyond a shadow of a doubt. As to what would happen after that... God only knew.

Fleming looked over at McDonald. The Specialist was standing stock-still, watching Byron with mournful eyes. To him, Fleming said, "McDonald, unless we get hit again, you're only duty is to remain with Sergeant Williamson. You are to remain with him until the bird arrives, and then see to it that he is onboard. Do you follow me, son?"

McDonald never took his eyes off Byron. "Roger that, Sergeant," was all his said. Fleming looked at Byron, who had managed to lay most of the pieces of the first little girl into roughly the right shape. "Fuck," he said, and went off to find the Convoy Commander. The after-action report on this would take *years*.

Chapter Seventeen

Byron finished speaking and the silence that followed was deafening. He thought he would have cried again, but it seemed that his ability to weep had been shut down, at least temporarily. He turned his head to look Bern in the eyes. Apparently, Bern had taken up the torch when it came to tears. They ran down his face unhindered and landed in his lap.

"Oh, son…" he said. "Oh son, I am so *sorry*…"

Byron smiled grimly. "I know, Father. You're sorry, I'm sorry, the whole world's sorry. It's just a sorry old world."

Bern looked at the man sitting beside him. To have gone through that, to have even *seen* that, losing his wife in a divorce, and now to have his daughter dying upstairs… what was keeping the man from losing his mind? To Byron he said, "Why didn't you come and talk to me before this? How long have you been carrying this around your neck like a stone? You did nothing wrong, you know."

That surprised Byron. "Did you miss the part where I told you I killed one of the men in my unit? I'm pretty sure I mentioned that. Fratricide is frowned upon in the modern military, Father."

Bern's eyes were glints of ice. "Yes, you did mention it. And let me tell you this, as a man of God. My only wish is probably the same one you have: that you would have killed that son of a bitch before he opened fire. Maybe I'm wrong. Maybe I'll spend the next few years doing nothing but penance for saying that… no, for *believing* that, but that's what I think. You are a paramedic. Your job is to save lives. Even in a war, your job was to save lives. You are a good man that terrible things have happened to, but that does not change the fact that *you are a good man, and you deserve to be happy!*"

Byron acted as he so often did, instinctively. He reached out and wrapped his arms around the older man's neck. Bern hugged him back, holding him tightly. Byron turned his head towards Bern's neck, catching a whiff of Old Spice, and whispered into his ear, "Thank you Father. Thank you for listening, and thank you for your forgiveness. But it doesn't matter. I am damned. I was damned the second I let that man die. To kill in defense of the innocent, I believe that is a forgivable sin. But to kill in hatred… no, I am damned. I accept that. But it will be *me* that's damned. They can't have Liza."

Bern pulled away, the confusion clear on his face. "But you didn't kill Henderson in hatred, son. You killed him to try to save innocent lives. You're not damned. If anyone is damned, it's Henderson, not you. You're not Sisyphus, son. Let the stone roll down the hill."

"I'm not talking about Henderson, Father. I'm talking about Dennis Schwacter. And that stone is never going to roll down the hill on my watch."

Byron rose from the pew, turned on his heel, and walked out of the chapel, and then the hospital. Father Bern sat in silence, his confusion complete.

Chapter Eighteen

Byron drove from the hospital back to his trailer. He parked in the side yard and stood looking at the shanty he had been living in. He would most definitively *not* miss this place. He went inside and looked around the living room. Had he actually been *living* like this? This was beyond filth, beyond neglect. There had been Iraqis living in mud brick buildings that were far cleaner and more livable that this. Something else he wasn't going to miss. He went to the fridge and opened it up. Once again, he was struck by the level of disgust that he felt. *Hell with it*, he thought *a day or two more and all of this is history.*

He went back into the living room and sat down on the couch. He closed his eyes and took several deep breaths. He opened them, looked around, and then said, "Okay, Schwacter. Let's get this over with." The only sound in the room was the ticking of the clock over the television. "Come on, big boy, no need to be shy, you son of a bitch."

"Okay, son. Here we are, let the games begin."

Byron looked around, but he didn't really expect to see anything. Apparently, the Schwacters of the paranormal world were only capable of being heard, not seen. That suited Byron right down to the ground, considering what Schwacter had looked like the last time he had seen the old fart.

"So," he said, "What now? Am I supposed to apologize? Beg forgiveness? Tell you that it was a terrible mistake and I should have never done it? Fine. Consider all that done, in spades. Whatever you need, whatever it takes for you to call of those kids from my little girl, and you've got it. Just say the word."

There was silence again, but a pensive silence. Byron could tell that Schwacter was thinking. After a few moments, the dead man spoke again.

"What are you rambling about, you motherfucker? Yeah, you killed me. We got that. What the hell are you going on about? I ain't *got* no kids, leastways none that I know about. And even if I did, how the hell would I get in touch with them to tell them to fuck with your little girl? You think there's a fucking pay phone from where I'm at? I don't even *know* where I'm at! I don't know where I am, and *I don't know what I'm supposed to do next*!!!" Schwacter's voice had taken on a shrill, panicky tone. "I'm dead, I know I'm dead. I watched my own goddamned funeral, and now I DON'T KNOW WHAT I'M SUPPOSED TO DO!!! YOU MOTHERFUCKER, WHAT DO I DO NOW???"

The mirror on the living room wall shattered into tiny shards. The frame trembled for a moment, and then came crashing down, as well. *Well, I guess he can do more than just* talk, *at that*, thought Byron. To

Schwacter he said, "Are you trying to tell me that you didn't get those little girls to come after Liza? It's just some big coincidence that the man I let die a week ago happens to start talking to me the same time that I start seeing kids that I know have been dead for years, right?"

This time Schwacter went all out. The refrigerator flew open and cans and bowls of congealed food flung itself across the room to splatter on the wall. The television screen imploded with a dull *crump*, leaving lead-colored pieces of glass lying all over the living room rug. The ceiling fan, although it had stopped working months before, now began to spin, faster and faster until it ripped itself off its mounting and shot through the air toward the couch. Had he not ducked, Byron was pretty sure that he would have been killed by a dead man. *'Killed by a Dead Man'*, he thought, *sounds like one of those new rock bands.*

Schwacter had either lost his ability to speak, or was just too far-gone in his fury to form words. The living room filled with a growing shriek that increased in volume to the point that Byron could feel his eardrums pressing in. The sound created a solid wave of pain that slammed him back into the couch. He screamed himself, but soundlessly, for there was no air left from the void created by Schwacter's fury.

Just as Byron was beginning to feel himself passing out, the sound began to abate. It tapered off to the level of a tea kettle whistle, then to a hiss, and then to a tiny movement of air. Byron sat up groggily, his head feeling like it weighed a thousand pounds. Although he could not feel it, blood was running in a constant stream from his nostrils and ears. One eye was filling with blood, as well. Like a drunken man, he staggered to his feet.

"That all you got, Schwacter?" he said, his voice sounding tinny and far-off in his ears. "You mess up my living room and throw some food around, and that's *it*? Hell, this place already looked like a pig sty; you think this makes any difference?"

It was quiet in the living room once again. Or at least Byron assumed it was quiet. The way his ears were ringing, there could have been a marching band in the bathroom playing "You Shook Me All Night Long" by AC/DC. He tried to walk back into the kitchen to get a glass of water, but after a couple of steps decided that sitting back down was the order of the day. Damn, he was in bad shape.

Just under the ringing, he heard Schwacter's voice one last time. "What do I do? Where do I go? It's cold and it's dark, and no one will *help* me!" As he spoke, Schwacter's voice faded out.

Byron lowered his head into his hands. "Schwacter, I don't know what to tell you. You're on your own. We're all on our own. If I had it to do over again, I would have tried to save your sorry ass, but I can't. I didn't kill you, I let you die. Maybe that's the same thing, maybe not. But I honestly don't know what to tell you to do. I thought you were the one fucking with my little girl, but it turns out you're not. So, you're dead and don't know what to do now, and I'm alive and don't know what to do now. There doesn't seem to be one whole hell of a lot of difference to me."

Silence. Even the ringing was beginning to subside. He ran his hands over his face and was surprised to find them covered with blood. After he felt like he could walk again, he stumbled to the bathroom. His nose and ears had stopped bleeding, but he still looked like he'd gone a few rounds with Mike Tyson if Mr. Tyson had decided to do some crystal meth and eat a handful of gunpowder He cleaned himself up as best he could and found a tee shirt that wasn't completely filthy. The rest of his clean clothes were at Amber's house. He'd have to go by there before he went back to the hospital. He didn't want Liza to see him looking like this. It would only upset her, and she had more than enough of that, thank you very much.

He went back out to his truck, working on a story to explain his blood-filled eye. He'd walked into a door? No, Christ, that was lame. He'd tripped coming down the steps of the house and hit himself in the eye on some of the concrete lawn edging? Yeah, that would work. The steps were unsteady as hell, and he actually *had* fallen a time or two. Mostly when he was drunk, sure, but he had fallen. That thought stopped him. When was the last time he had had anything to drink? That wine at Amber's? He gave a little grin at his image in the rearview mirror. *Hey Liza, guess what? I think Daddy's on the wagon!*

He reversed out onto the street and drove towards Amber's house to fetch some clean clothes.

He never came back to his trailer again.

Chapter Nineteen

No one was home at Amber's. Her Toyota Highlander was in the drive, but no one answered the door. He got the spare key from the stupid little garden gnome and let himself in. Stacked on top of the dryer were all his clothes, neatly folded. He felt a wave of warmth for her flow over him. He placed his clean clothes into a garbage bag, being careful not to undo her folding, and then went into the kitchen. He planned to write her a note telling her thanks for his clothes, for the dinner, and for just being her. When he got to the fridge, he found that there was already a note there. Written in her back-handed cursive, she had stuck it on the fridge under a magnet from Gatlinburg.

Byron,

Your clothes are on the dryer. They are folded so DO NOT JUST THROW THEM IN A BAG!!! There is some left-over veggie lasagna in the fridge if you want it. Eat it, cuz I know I can't finish it all. I've gone to Wally World with Linda and Susan. Girl's night out in Dawkin's Mill, can I possibly stand the excitement??? I called to check on Liza before I left, and gave the charge nurse my pager #. If you need anything, you've got my cell #. I should be back home around 8 or 9. If you're not here, I'll check the hospital.

I love you, Big Guy,

Amber

(P.S. Last night was something I've wanted for a very long time. Maybe next time we might try it with our clothes off, what do you think? Loves- Amber)

Byron read the note twice, his eyes misting with tears. Seems like the boys at the waterworks factory were back in business. He took the note off the fridge and held it to his nose, like he had seen soldiers do in the field, hoping to get a whiff of the love they had left back home.

He folded the letter and stuck in his back pocket, then went into the bathroom to splash some water on his face and try to comb his hair out. He wanted to look at least quasi-presentable when he got the hospital. He turned on the bathroom light and stood staring at the sink. The tears put in their appearance, back for another stunning run. Amber had gone out and bought him shaving cream and a razor, deodorant and aftershave. They were lined up in a neat little row. He wiped his eyes and cleaned himself up.

As he was pulling on a clean shirt, he decided. He had put it off long enough. His certainty that Schwacter had been the driving force behind Liza's sudden turn for the worse had prepared him to do whatever was necessary to make amends. Now that he was certain that Schwacter hadn't had a hand in it, it was time for some professional help. Byron didn't discount what had happened at his trailer. He had the hemorrhaged eye to prove that something had happened. He also wasn't the type of person to see something inexplicable, and then move heaven and earth trying to come up with a logical reason for it. He had seen those little girls, just as he had heard Schwacter's voice. It had happened. That was okay. He could handle that. He could handle it as long as he had the one thing that had been eluding him so long he had forgotten it existed. He could handle it if he had hope.

Just hope.

Chapter Twenty

Byron walked into Sacred Hearts and was met before he could clear the lobby by Tiffany Brown. She had a harried look in her eyes and grabbed him by the arm and pulled him into the waiting room. After making sure they were alone, she said, "Rutherford's looking for you. He's waiting for you to come in. He says that you've finally done it, because you've missed three days' work in a row. He says it's out of his hands, because the hospital board has it in their policy and procedure manual that any employee that misses three or more days in a row without an excuse is subject to immediate dismissal."

Byron was sure that the wording of the manual was exactly what Tiffany had said, verbatim. Tiffany had forgotten more about the bureaucracy that made this place tick than most of the department heads had ever learned in the first place. He told Tiffany that it was okay, that he figured his days were numbered at Sacred Heart. Tiffany grinned like a little girl. The effect was nothing short of amazing.

"Nope, you're days are most certainly *not* numbered, Ram. You want to know why? Because I submitted a Leave of Absence form with your signature on it *two days ago*!"

Byron's jaw dropped. "You did *what*??? Tiffany, they can fire you for that! You've got to get that thing out of the file before Rutherford finds it!"

"Nope! Nope, nope, nope! It's filed; it's signed, by *you*, and counter-signed by *me*, who happens to do scheduling for our lovely little department!"

"But... Tiff, *how*??? I may have been pretty jacked up in the head, but I'm pretty sure that I would have remembered signing a Leave of Absence form."

Tiffany gave him a look that said *I didn't fall off the hay truck yesterday, buddy-boy.* "Ram, how many run sheets do you think you turn it to me a week? And what's on the bottom of each one?"

Byron's capacity for shock seemed to be bottomless. "Do you mean to tell me that you *forged* my signature??? *You*???"

Tiffany looked slightly abashed. Then, defensively, she said, "Yes, Mr. Byron Williamson, *me*. I didn't figure you would remember to do it yourself, so I did it for you."

Shift whistle for the boys in the waterworks factory, time to get to it, Byron thought. Tears rolled down his face. Tiffany looked alarmed, but calmed down when Byron hugged her around the neck.

"Thank you so much, Tiffany. I never even thought to do something like that. With everything that has been going on with Liza, it never crossed my mind. To be honest, I don't think I really cared.

But Tiffany, why would you do something like this? They could fire you, at the very least. I don't want you losing your job on account of me."

Tiffany looked at Byron with an absent kind of fondness. "I don't care for some of the crap you pull, Ram, and you know it. Drinking on the job, *not* acceptable. But it would take a blind person not see how bad you're hurting. You are on hell of a medic. Sacred needs you. Once Liza gets better, you'll see. Things will start to turn around."

"Tiffany, how can I thank you? What can I do? You're right; once Liza gets out of here she's going to need a Daddy that's not drawing unemployment. Not to mention Robbie. What can I do to make this right with you?"

"You can go upstairs and see your little girl, that's what you can do. Make her smile. Tell her you love her. And then, I want you to go somewhere and get yourself together. No more booze, Ram. That crap doesn't help. Deal?"

Byron stuck out his hand. "You have a deal, Ms. Brown."

Tiffany slapped his hand away, laughing. "Go on, you dummy. And remember, you turned in that leave form two days ago. Anything else and you'll get me in trouble. Got it?"

"Yes, Ma'am, I read you five-by-five."

Tiffany rolled her eyes. "Whatever *that* means," she muttered. She was already moving down the hall, preparing to deal with the myriad of problems that plagued the EMS department, problems only she was capable of working out.

Byron headed for the stairs. He ran up the three flights to the I.C.U. unit, and was slightly ashamed that it had winded him. *I have got to get myself back in shape. The boys in the 3rd would laugh me out of the room.* A slight grimace crossed his face at the thought. He had tried very hard to put the time he spent in Army out of his mind. He had enjoyed Army life in general, its structure appealing to his nature. Lately, however, it seemed that his involvement in the Iraqi war seemed to be playing a bigger and bigger part in his life, whether he liked it or not.

He walked down the hallway towards Liza's room, his mind rolling back to his last, hazy days as a Sergeant in the United States Army.

Chapter Twenty-One

The Blackhawk flared into the LZ, a fine grit of sand and debris scouring the earth around it. The men of the convoy were loading the wounded onto it before it came fully to rest. Specialist McDonald, true to his word, had not been more than five feet from Byron since the horrific events that followed the brief firefight. Byron had managed to assemble almost all the pieces of the children into their proper place. What was left was the most pitiful thing McDonald had ever seen.

Byron sat brushing one girl's hair back from her brow. The rounds had left this child's face unmarked, and she appeared to be asleep, provided her face was all you looked at. Byron had been speaking to the children's bodies in a low, soothing voice until the roar of the Blackhawk had drowned him out.

He looked up irritably when he heard the bird coming in, and then he smiled. He jumped up and sprinted back to his Humvee. McDonald sprinted right along with him. Byron opened the Humvee door, and was rummaging around inside. He never spared a glance at Henderson, lying beside the Humvee on the road in a partially open body bag. As he poked around in the back of the Humvee, two soldiers from the convoy came up and grasped the bag by the handles and carried it toward the waiting Blackhawk. The medic that had come in with the bird took a quick look at Henderson, shook his head, and thumbed the men to place the body in the Blackhawk.

Byron had finally found what he was looking for, and took the bundle with him back to the children. McDonald followed, loyal as the family dog. Once Byron had reached the children, he began unrolling his bundle, which turned out to be three tarps. He laid one beside each body and began the delicate process of transporting the pieces onto the tarp. McDonald merely stood silently, watching.

Byron had finished with the first child, and was halfway done with the second when First Sergeant Fleming arrived, the convoy commander in tow. The commander was a Captain named Leonard. He stood beside Fleming, the men silently watching Byron as he continued his grisly task. After several moments, Captain Leonard looked over at Fleming.

"Sweet Jesus-*fuck*, First Sergeant."

Fleming nodded. "Yes, Sir, that's about what I thought. The question now is what the hell do we do with him?"

The Captain slid his Kevlar back on his head and wiped the sweat off his brow. "Well, the first thing we do is get down on our ever-loving knees and thank God and all his Apostles that we didn't have a reporter embedded with us, or this shit would be playing live on CNN right now."

Fleming nodded again. "Roger that, sir, thanking God and all his Apostles that we didn't have an embedded reporter with us. However, seeing as we didn't, Sir, the question remains." He held one hand out toward Byron, as if that should be self-evident.

The Captain stood silently for a moment, and then turned to Fleming. "This is our medic, right? Williams?"

"Williamson, Sir, Sergeant Byron Williamson."

"I don't give a fuck if his name is Robert E. Motherfucking Lee, First Sergeant, is he our medic, or is he not?"

"Yes, Sir."

The Captain nodded. "All right. The man is quite obviously not capable of carrying out his duties. You take him over to that Blackhawk and get their medic. Tell him he just got drafted into the 3rd Infantry until further notice. If he, or any of the other flyboys give you any grief about it, tell 'em that unless one of 'em is a General, I don't wanna hear it. Take Sergeant Williamson over and place him on the bird." Leonard struck his palm against the side of his helmet. "Ah, *Christ*, we need somebody that was here and knows what the fuck happened to go with him. We can't just turn his ass loose at the FOB to wander around. And no, before you volunteer, you can't go, First Sergeant; I need your ass right here. *Shit!*"

"I'll take him, Sir", said a quiet voice.

Captain Leonard turned to McDonald. "You were in his vehicle?"

"Yes, Sir. I witnessed the entire episode."

Leonard laughed disgustedly. "'Episode'. Right. Well, fuck it, you're volunteered then. However, you are not to speak to *anyone* about this shit, do you understand? I don't care if George W. Bush happens to be back at the Forward Operating Base and wants to know what's going on, you're to just smile and say, 'I have no idea, Mr. President. I was ordered to remain with Sergeant Williamson. Please direct any further inquiries to Captain James S. Leonard, 2nd Brigade, 3rd Infantry Division, currently in Fallujah, Iraq. Got all that, Specialist?"

"Yes, Sir. I got it."

"All right then. Let's see if we can separate Sergeant Williamson from his new playmates, then." He ran a hand over his sweaty face and shook his head in disgust. "Fuck me. I should have been a lawyer, like my dad wanted."

Between the three of them, they managed to get Byron onto the Blackhawk, and then only by promising that the children were being evacuated to a special Children's Intensive Care Facility on the outskirts of Baghdad for treatment. That no such facility existed was not something they chose to share with Byron. The Blackhawk medic wasn't very pleased by the news that he was now the acting medic for the convoy, but changed his tune when Fleming threatened to "beat his eyeballs out of his asshole". The look on Fleming's face had convinced the flight medic that the First Sergeant was a man of his word.

The flight crew was informed that Sergeant Williamson was to be taken to the infirmary when they arrived, to be placed under guard, and to be given an immediate psychological evaluation. Specialist McDonald was his escort, and would be accompanying them. The flight crew looked at the body bag containing Henderson and the several moaning Iraqi civilians loaded into the back of their aircraft and said nothing more. The Blackhawk ascended into the hot Iraqi sun and headed back towards Baghdad.

As they stood watching the bird disappear into the distance, Fleming looked at Captain Leonard and asked, "How the hell are we gonna write this thing up, Sir?"

The Captain stared off into the distance for a moment, and then turned.

"We write it up just like it happened, Sergeant. Do you honestly think we could make up anything anymore fucked than this already is?"

First Sergeant Fleming looked at the Captain and said nothing.

Unable to bear the First Sergeant's gaze, Leonard finally said, "Okay, what *I* see here is an unfortunate incident that resulted in the deaths of three Iraqi civilians during an ambush. What I *also* see is that during that same ambush, an American soldier was accidentally killed in a friendly-fire exchange. Does that coincide with what you saw?"

The First Sergeant looked at the carnage around him for a long moment before he answered.

"Yes, sir, that's pretty much exactly how the shit went down from my perspective."

Leonard nodded. "Okay, then, let's get this fucking convoy moving. I want to be set up in a defensive position before another hour goes by." He turned and prepared to leave when Fleming spoke.

"And the bodies of the civilians, sir? We going to just leave them here beside the road?

Leonard turned an unhealthy shade of purple under his Kevlar. "God-*dammit*, First Sergeant! What would you suggest? A candlelight memorial? We've got a mission, and that isn't it!"

Fleming remained unruffled in the face of this outburst. He had been chewed out by officers of *much* high rank than Leonard before, and for much less reason. When he replied, his voice was soft.

"Never mind, sir. I'll take a detail of men out and find the girls' parents. It won't take long. And I'm sure that that they will appreciate the care and consideration the United States Army is taking by finding them so they can bury their children properly. It's a shame that those girls missed all the democracy we're bringing to their country, isn't it, sir?"

With that, Fleming snapped off a salute and went to find a detail of men for the grisly task at hand. Leonard stood, hands on hips, staring at the departing back of his First Sergeant. The look of fury on his face soon dissolved into one of sorrow. With a sad shake of his head, he moved up the convoy. He had a perimeter to set up.

Onboard the Blackhawk, Byron busied himself on the ride to Baghdad by treating the minor wounds on the Iraqi civilians, cleaning and debriding the lacerations, then wrapping them in gauze. Once he had them taken care of, he looked over towards the body bag containing Henderson. Reaching over, he pulled the bag open and looked down into Henderson's face. He looked over at McDonald in confusion.

"When did Henderson get zipped?"

McDonald just looked calmly back at Byron.

"Dunno, Sarge. Must have been during the ambush, I suppose."

Byron examined the body, at one point asking McDonald to help him remove Henderson's body armor. Looking at the wounds, Byron's expression grew confused. He looked at McDonald and said, "These look like 5.56 wound patterns. But the angle is all wrong. Looks like he got hit at least four, maybe five times, but all the entry wounds are coming in from *under* his armor. Look at the exit wounds. How the hell did *that* happen?"

McDonald continued to stare calmly at Byron. "Like I said, Sarge, I dunno. I was covering my sector. Didn't see anything else. It got kinda lively there for a minute."

Byron nodded and spent the rest of the trip looking out at the passing desert, occasionally throwing a confused glance at the body of Private Matthew Henderson.

<u>Chapter Twenty-Two</u>

Byron came to himself and realized he had been standing in front of Liza's door for several moments. He looked furtively up and down the hall, ensuring that no one was wondering if the tall idiot in the hallway was lost or not. With an embarrassed grin, he opened to door and entered the room.

Samantha was asleep in one of the lounge chairs that hospitals manage to order from some mediaeval torture company in Europe. Impossible to find any comfort, you eventually just passed out in them from pure exhaustion. Samantha had a hospital blanket draped over her and was snoring softly. Byron glanced over at Liza's bed, and was surprised to see that she was awake and looking at him with a smile. He grinned back.

"Mommy's asleepun," she stage whispered to him.

"I can see that she is, kiddo," he whispered back.

"Mommy is *snoring*," she said, and then giggled.

"Like an elephant," Byron agreed, trying not to laugh himself.

"A *biiiiggg* helefunt," she said, now giggling loudly.

"A ginormous one," he agreed again, and now he lost it himself.

They were both trying to smother their laughter, snorting and blowing, when Samantha woke up and looked at them, startled. "What? What is it?" she asked, confusion evident on her sleep-puffy face.

Byron, tears now rolling down his face, tried to get control over himself. "Liza and I were just discussing pachyderms," he said, trying to keep a straight face. However, at the word "pachyderms", Liza broke up again, which caused Byron to go off into gales of laughter.

Samantha looked at them suspiciously. "You two are both *very* silly," she said. She straightened up and stretched her arms above her head, giving a jaw-cracking yawn. She looked around groggily and asked Byron what time it was.

Byron looked at his watch. "It's a little after seven," he told her.

"You're not supposed to be here until eight," she said, giving him a sour glance. "From eight to eight, that was the deal."

Byron sighed. "I was up, so I figured I'd come on by. No harm, no foul. If you want to go on home and take a shower or whatever, I'm here. I don't mind."

"I'll leave at eight o'clock," she said sharply. "Not at seven-fifty-five, not at eight-oh-five, eight o'clock. Got that?"

Byron held up his hands. "Got it, Samantha. Eight o'clock, no problem. I'll go down to the cafeteria and get a cup of coffee or something."

"Something, sure. Maybe a little shot in your coffee, you know, just to get the day going?" Samantha said venomously.

"Sam, not in front of the baby, all right? Please? Liza, Daddy will be back in a little while, okay?"

Liza, who had been watching this exchange with a frightened look, nodded vigorously. "'Kay, Daddy. When you come back will you 'n Mommy not have no more bad-fights?"

Byron winced, and saw Samantha do the same. "I promise, baby. No more bad-fights. Right, Mommy?"

Samantha nodded. "Mommy's sorry, angel. I guess I just woke up on the wrong side of the bed this morning."

"You's not in a bed, Mommy. You's in a chair."

Samantha smiled. "Right, angel. I woke up on the wrong side of the *chair* this morning."

Byron turned to go. He glanced at Samantha. "Eight o'clock. I'm sorry for being early. Do you want me to bring either of you anything from the cafeteria when I come back?"

Samantha shook her head. "We're fine. Eight o'clock." With that, she dismissed him from her mind.

Byron felt the old anger start to rise up, but he crushed it down resolutely. He had to remember that this was hard on Samantha, too. He just nodded and left the room.

He walked back down the stairs to the ground floor, heading for the cafeteria. He was about to enter the door when he was stopped by the gloating voice of Donald Rutherford, M.D.

"Excuse *me*, Mr. Williamson, but I'm afraid you'll have to accompany me to my office. It appears that the department has had to intervene concerning your excessive absences."

Byron turned to Rutherford. He pasted an innocent and confused look on his face and then asked mildly, "And what excessive absences would those be, *Don?*"

Rutherford sneered. "You know damned well what absences I mean. You have not reported for work for three consecutive days, which is against departmental regulations. As this is your third write-up in a four month period, I'm afraid the department has decided to let you go."

"The *department* has decided to let me go, huh? Wow, that really hurts, Don. I mean after all we've been through together, the close bonds formed by our mutual love of the medical field, and all that, it just really cuts me to the bone."

"Yes, I'm sure it does, Williamson. Before you go off making your threats, just you know that this wasn't *my* decision to make. The department heads have written those protocols for a reason, and anyone that deviates from them is subject to dismissal. I'm not the one doing the firing here, Williamson. That needs to be clear here. I have nothing to do with it."

"Really, Don? If you have nothing to do with it, why are *you* the one breaking your neck to give me this splendid news at the crack of dawn?"

Rutherford sputtered. "Well, I felt it was my duty to convey their decision to you. I *am* the head of the EMS department, after all."

"Yes, you are. However, it has been my experience that employment and dismissal is usually done by Human Resources, not the department head. Furthermore, Human Resources doesn't usually come in until at least eight, seeing as that's when the department opens, and even then sometimes they don't arrive until eight-thirty, quarter to nine. So, at the risk of repeating myself and sounding like a simpleton, I'm afraid I must ask again, why are *you* telling me this first thing in the morning? Especially if, as you have so clearly pointed out you have nothing to do with it?"

Rutherford adopted a martyred stance. "Look, Byron, I'm just trying to let you know what is happening. I figured the sooner you knew, the sooner you could begin looking for other employment. You'll need an income, after all." Suddenly, he dropped the attitude and stared straight into Byron's eyes. "You hate me. I hate you. Fine, we're clear on that. As far as that little... *incident* with those pills, I just want you to know that there is no more of that sort of thing going on. I've stopped it completely. I also got Dr. Pyrrus to see Elizabeth as a professional courtesy to me. You won't see a bill from him at all. On top of that, I will write you a sterling letter of recommendation to wherever you apply for a new job. You can tell them whatever you want as to why you left here. I'll gloss over the problems we've had, and you'll be back in business. I'm sure that Dawkins Methodist would be glad to have you. However, I want you out of my hospital. I'm not going to lie about that. I want you gone, today. Of course, you will be free to come and go to see Elizabeth, but I want your locker cleared out and your identification badge turned in to my office by the end of business hours, today. Are we clear on all that? I think, with the situation being what it is, that I'm being extremely fair about all of this. So, are you going to go quietly, or is this going to become a scene? Because I warn you, Williamson, I will not hesitate to have security escort you from this building, your threats be damned." Rutherford's voice had steadily risen throughout this last rant.

Byron was amazed at how calm he had remained in the face of this. A few days ago, he would have already have been beating this little weasel into the ground. *Maybe I* am *getting better*, he thought. To Rutherford, he said, "Well, Don, I appreciate you being as honest and up-front with me as you have been, so I am going to return that courtesy to you. There are some slight problems with the scenario as you've just lain it out. First, I feel compelled to remind you that this is not *your* hospital. All doctors have a bit of a God complex; that comes with the job. You, however, seem to have a complete pantheon complex. If your ego gets any bigger, it's going to start developing its own weather patterns. Secondly, according to the policy and procedure manual that I read when I was hired here, excessive absences are, and I quote: 'Any absences of three or more days without a doctor's excuse or a leave of absence form filled out and turned in to the scheduling department.' Does that sound about correct, *Doctor* Rutherford?"

Rutherford laughed. "If you think that *I'm* going to write you an excuse, you're sadly mis-"

Byron overrode him. "No, Don, I don't expect you to write me an excuse. I wouldn't expect you to write me an excuse if my legs were blown off while saving one of your children from an exploding car. Which is why I filled out a leave of absence form and turned it in two *days* ago."

Rutherford stood gaping like a landed trout. "What... I mean, when... how....who..."

Byron laughed. "All you need is 'where' and you've got yourself a news story, Don. Let me say this again, very slowly and in words of few syllables, so that you will understand, okay? I turned in a leave of absence form two days ago. That's forty-eight hours. A leave of absence form. Turned in. Are you tracking me now, Don? Have I left anything out, or not explained it clearly enough for you?"

Rutherford shook like an old dog. "*Bullshit!*" he nearly screamed. "You did no such thing! If there was such a form turned in, it would be on file, and I didn't see one!"

"I thought you had nothing to do with this, Don," Byron said, his voice silky. "What were you doing going through my EMS file is you have no dog in this race, hmm?"

"I'm the goddamned head of the EMS department! I can go through those files whenever I feel like it! If you've filled out a leave of absence form, who did you get to counter-sign it? I know *I* sure as hell didn't!"

"I turned in a properly signed form to Ms. Tiffany Brown, head of scheduling in the EMS department two days ago. She signed it, and told me that she would arrange shift coverage for me. Due to my daughter's illness, I was unsure of how much time I might need, so I filled out an open-ended form. Tiffany said we would revisit it in a week or so, and see how Liza was doing, and then go from there."

Rutherford had turned an ugly plum color, and was breathing in a shallow, rapid way. He opened his mouth several times, but could find nothing to say, and closed it. Finally, he spun on his heel and stalked down the hallway.

"You should get your blood pressure checked, Don," Byron called after him. "Hypertension is the silent killer, you know!"

Rutherford didn't respond, and slammed through the doors at the end of the hall. Byron chuckled and then silently sent Tiffany Brown another heart-felt thank you. Even keeping his job was secondary to just being able to piss Donald Rutherford off. When the two things coincided, it was a grand day, indeed. Still smiling, he walked into the cafeteria to get himself a cup of coffee.

<u>Chapter Twenty-Three</u>

Byron spent the day with Liza. She slept much of the time, due to the morphine, but otherwise, they had a fine time. Every so often, Byron would look over at her and say "pachyderm", which would invariably lead to a fit of the giggles. They watched several hours of Teletubbies, and Byron taught her how to play checkers. After beating him four times in a row, Liza began to suspect he was throwing the games. "If you's not gonna play right, I don't wanna play wif you, Daddy," she informed him in a prim little voice. He laughed, and said that he was just having an off day, but tomorrow he would beat her every game. She agreed, but by around three in the afternoon, she told him that she was getting tired and wanted a nap. Byron told her that was fine, and he tucked her in with her stuffed animals, placing her favorite teddy bear next to her on the pillow. He asked her if she would be all right if he ran downstairs while she was napping, and she said that was fine. He kissed her on the forehead and told her loved her, but she was already asleep.

Byron told the nurse at the desk that he had to run downstairs, and for her to page him when Liza woke up, if she didn't mind. She agreed, and he went back down the stairs to the ground floor again. He went past Rutherford's office, but thankfully, the man wasn't in. Byron had no desire to have another chat with Rutherford. He had other things to do today. Byron continued down the hallway until he came to a door marked "Dr. Michael Franklin". Dr. Franklin was the hospital's psychiatrist. Byron had studiously avoided this man for several months, but he figured this meeting was long overdue. With a mental sigh, he knocked on the door.

Michael Franklin was a small, spare man with a head full of wavy ash-blonde hair. He had an engaging smile, and Byron detected none of the self-important righteousness he had encountered with previous psychiatrists. Even with his initial misgivings, he found himself liking the man.

"Call me Mike," Franklin said as he gestured Byron into a seat. "You're Byron Williamson, right? The one everybody calls 'Ram'"? I've heard good things about you. They tell me you are one hell of a medic. Did you really threaten to run over somebody's car when they wouldn't get out of the way?"

Inundated with all these rapid-fire questions, Byron laughed and held up his hands. "One thing at a time, Doc, what do you say?"

Franklin laughed too. "Sorry. I'm kinda mouthy; at least that's what the wife tells me. I'm just a garrulously social animal, what can I say?"

"Well, Doc, let's see: Yes, my name is Byron, and yes, everyone calls me 'Ram'. As far as being a good medic, I try my best. And, yes, I did threaten to run over a car. Insofar as you hearing good things about me… well, you obviously haven't been talking to my department head."

Franklin flapped a hand. "Rutherford? I'm not sure I'd believe that little shit if he told me that the sun had shown up in the eastern quadrant of the sky this morning without checking to make sure myself."

Byron barked out a laugh. "You know, Doc, I think I'm gonna like you."

"Well, most folks do, once they get past what I do for a living. So, what brings you in to see me today?"

Byron gave the man a sly glance. "I'm pretty sure you know why I'm here better than I do, Doc."

"Well, maybe I do, and maybe I don't. What I do know is, I want to know why *you* came to see me, not why anyone else thinks you should."

Byron thought a moment. He wasn't sure what he had intended to tell this man. Once he began speaking, he was amazed to find himself telling him everything that had happened. He watched Franklin's reaction carefully when he told him about the little girls in the road, and later in Liza's room, and about Schwacter's little redecorating job of his trailer, but the man never changed his attentive posture. He also didn't take the first note, something that surprised Byron. He had figured the man would have been scribbling madly.

When he had finished talking, he looked at Franklin. "Well, Doc, do I need to make a reservation for a rubber room, or what?

Franklin surprised him by saying "I don't know. Do *you* think you do?"

Byron blew out an exasperated breath. "Are you one of those shrinks that answers every question with another question? That *kills* me."

"Nope, I genuinely want to know if you think you need to be institutionalized."

"Well hell, Doc, *I* don't know. You're the shrink. I figure you'd be the better judge of that than I would."

Franklin leaned forward. "You know what I see sitting in front of me? I see a very intelligent man that has been put through some shit I wouldn't even want to have to think about. Your military experience alone is enough to permanently scar most people. You get through that, and now you have this to deal with. A divorce and a child with a terrible disease. You think anyone faced with that wouldn't feel ready for a padded room somewhere?"

"So you *do* think I need to go somewhere, then?"

"Sure I do. I think you need to go your local pharmacy and fill the prescriptions I'm about to write for you. And then I think you need to spend as much time as you can with your little girl. But *balance* your time. Get some sleep. A decent meal. You have to relax at some point, or you'll be of no use to your little girl or anyone else. These meds will help with that, but they aren't magical cure-alls. You've got to work on making sure you keep yourself on an even keel. You follow me, here? I take it you aren't working right now, right?"

"No, I'm on a leave of absence."

"Okay, good. Then some of the stuff I write you will be a little strong at first. You won't be a zombie, or anything, but it will help you to relax. In addition to that, you need to come and see me on a fairly regular basis for a while. Don't worry, I'm not one of these 'Let's rehash every event since childhood' kind of psychiatrists. You have a fairly good handle on what's happened to you in your life. I see no need in bringing it back up every other day."

Byron hesitated, and then said, "What about the little girls? About Schwacter? I mean, do you think I'm hallucinating all that stuff? Because let me tell you, Doc, my living room looks like a monster truck drove through it."

Franklin thought about it for a moment, his fingers lightly touching each other in front of him. "Here's the thing, Byron. Most of the folks in my field would tell you that you were, in fact, hallucinating all of this. They would further tell you that in the grips of that hallucination, you destroyed your *own* living room, and have no memory of it. Me, I don't know. Just because I didn't see it, doesn't meant that it didn't happen. There are stranger things than I ever thought of going on all the time. I may not understand them, but that doesn't mean that I deny them."

Byron took the final plunge. "Okay. One more thing. I've told you about Schwacter. I let that man die. In the eyes of the State of Tennessee, I am guilty of manslaughter, at the very least. You know about it, and that makes you an accessory after the fact if you don't report it. I know all about patient confidentiality, but this goes a bit past all that, don't you think?"

Franklin stared out his window. He was quiet for so long, Byron was beginning to wish he hadn't asked the question. He was about to say something, anything, to fill the void when Franklin spoke.

"What you've told me concerning Dennis Schwacter is this: You responded to a call, and you transported a patient to the hospital. That patient was declared dead on arrival by the E.R. physician. Now, insofar as what happened in the back of that ambulance, how am I supposed to know if you purposefully withheld medical treatment from that man? We are talking about a man that admits to seeing ghosts, after all. Maybe you hallucinated what happened with Schwacter. Look, Ram. I've seen your medical file from the Army. I know what went down, at least the military version of what went down. The fact that you fired upon one of your fellow soldiers weighed quite heavily on the outcome of that ambush. You know the deal, I'm sure you read the thing. They ruled it a friendly-fire fratricide. The men in the vehicle confirmed it. Your weapon went off while you were exiting the vehicle to respond to the wounded civilians. Now, that's what the *Army* says. What *you* say is that you shot Private Henderson and subsequently forgot about it until much later on. Which is it? Did you willfully shoot Henderson? If so, I applaud you for it. I just wish you had managed to do it before he killed anyone. With Schwacter, *you* say you withheld medical treatment. *I* say the man died as a result of a lifetime of alcohol abuse that his body simply couldn't handle."

Byron was thunderstruck. He simply sat, staring off into space until Franklin snapped his fingers in front of his eyes several times and said, "Still with me there, Ram?"

Byron jerked, and looked at Franklin. "Yes sir, present and accounted for. It's just that you're not the first person to tell me that they wished I would have popped Henderson quicker than I did. I just don't understand why so many people go so far out of their way to cover for me. To try to take care of me. You, Amber, Tiffany, Father Bern, hell, the guys in my unit… why are you all so willing to place yourselves at risk for me?"

Franklin had picked up a file and was flipping through it when he glanced over at Byron and said, "Have you ever considered the possibility that you are a good man, and that people can tell that about you? That those same people can recognize your inherent decency and respond to it? Ah, from the look in your eyes, I can see not. Have a good day, Ram. Kiss your little girl for me. I'm just going to call these prescriptions in to the hospital pharmacy. You can probably pick them up by five or so. I'll talk to you again tomorrow. If you need anything in the meantime, my number's on the back of that card I gave you. I'm an insomniac, so don't worry about waking me up. Later, bro,"

With that, Franklin bent to his file. Byron left his office feeling like he'd been hit by a sledge hammer made out of chloroform. Franklin was absolutely right. The possibility that people were looking out for him because he was a good man had never even entered his mind.

It hadn't entered his mind because he had never even considered the possibility that he was a good man.

Chapter Twenty-Four

He spent the rest of the day with Liza, mostly watching her sleep. He found himself mesmerized by the tiny veins around her eyes, the flutter of her breath. It felt like he could spend the rest of his life happily staring at his little girl.

Love isn't easy, he thought. *It's just about the hardest goddamned thing that there is. But no matter how much pain... all of it... it all comes down to moments like this one. Just me and my little girl. I can't rip the leukemia out of her and strangle it, as much as I may want to. I can't protect her from it like I could a bad person. I can't control this. I can't fix this. But, oh God, how I love her. Please, God. I know You're probably sick of hearing prayers like this one. I'm not making any deals. It doesn't work that way, I understand that. You probably wouldn't want to make a deal with somebody like me in the first place. I mentally threatened to knock you down and kick your teeth out the other day. But I would take her place in an instant if You would let me, but I know that's not the way it goes. So, no deals. I'm just asking you. No, I'm fucking begging you... don't take my little girl. Please.*

He had no idea if his odd little prayer had worked, especially since he had pretty much given up on the whole concept of God since Iraq. But as a father, he had to cover all his bases. He might be

171

committing blasphemy just talking to a God he wasn't sure existed, but that's what you do when you are a father. You cover those bases.

Liza woke up again around seven-thirty, something for which Byron was profoundly thankful. He had been terribly afraid that she would sleep through the rest of his time, and wouldn't wake up until after Samantha ran him out of here at eight. She stretched her little arms and looked around.

"Daddy?" she asked.

"Yes, baby?"

"Why are my new-best friends not here? They's here when I went to sleepun, but they's not here now."

Byron smiled at her. "They probably had to go home for a while. Their Mommies and Daddies would miss them, too, you know. Just like I miss you when you're not with me."

"No, they's not with their Mommies and Daddies. They telled me that their Mommies and Daddies don't live in Heaven yet. They telled me that they'd help me find Heaven when it was time. So I won't getted lost."

Gooseflesh broke out all over Byron's body. It was a huge struggle, but he managed to keep his smile in place. His voice was pleasant when he answered her.

"Liza, do you remember what Daddy said about not going anywhere with those little girls?"

"Yes, Daddy. You told me not to go nowhere's with them, no matter what."

"That's right, baby. Daddy means that. You don't go with them, even if they ask you to."

"But why, Daddy? If I go with them, they told me I won' hurt no more. I don't wanna hurt no more."

Byron's reserve was cracking. No one would ever know the effort it took to keep that smile on his face.

"I know, sweetheart. I don't want you to hurt any more, either. But Daddy thinks that if you go with those girls, then I won't be able to see you anymore, and that would break Daddy's heart. I can't go without seeing my baby girl, you know."

Liza smiled. "It's okay, Daddy. My new-best friends told me that you will see me in Heaven."

"Well, that's good that we'll be together in Heaven, baby. But let's just stay here for now, okay? Besides, we've still got to go fishing, remember? You've got to get feeling better. Those fish aren't going to catch themselves, you know."

Liza yawned. The morphine that was keeping her from being in agony was also keeping her almost constantly tired. She smiled sleepily up at Byron. "I still don't think there's fishies bigger'n Daddy," she said. Her eyes slid closed again and her soft respiration was the only sound in the room.

"Bigger than Daddy, baby girl. Lots bigger than Daddy. And we're going to catch every one of them."

He sat staring raptly at his daughter until Samantha came in at eight. She asked him how Liza had been that day, and then told him it was time for him to go. He rose, planted a gentle kiss on Liza's sleeping brow, and walked out of the room. He went down the stairs and by the hospital pharmacy. The pharmacist working the window asked him how Liza was doing and told him if he needed anything at all, just to let her know. Byron thanked her, again amazed by the fact that these people that he really didn't know honestly seemed to care about his life. Hell, he couldn't remember what the pharmacist's name was that had given him his prescriptions.

He walked out into the night air and stopped by his truck. It was only then that he realized that he had no idea where he was going. Back to the trailer? No, thank you. He'd rather check into a damned motel than go back to that place. He climbed into his truck and started driving. He was almost all the way to Amber Jennson's house before he realized he was even going there.

<u>Chapter Twenty-Five</u>

Amber met him at the door wearing a tee shirt that looked like a dress on her. Her hair was pulled back into a pony tail. She hugged him and then kissed him on the mouth, hard. When she pulled back, she was a little breathless.

"I wasn't sure you were coming back tonight," she said. "You didn't call or leave a note." There was no reproach in her voice, just relief that he was there. He felt guilty as hell about not leaving a note.

"I meant to write you a note and put it on the fridge, but I found yours and I just…" he shrugged helplessly.

She grinned at him. "Well, come on in here and let's see what we're going to eat."

Despite his protests, she insisted on making dinner for him. He was quite qualified to cook for himself, thank you very much, he told her. She told him that was fine by her; he was in charge of peeling potatoes.

"Great," he growled. "Now I'm on K.P."

They worked well together in the kitchen. Whenever she needed something, he always seemed to have it in hand, and vice versa.

They talked about old times while they cooked, about people they had gone to school with and where those people had ended up.

"Do you remember Mary Caldwell?" she asked, transferring pieces of fried chicken onto a paper-towel covered plate.

He thought for a moment and then said, "You mean the girl that banged the whole basketball team?"

She slapped at him. "That's a very crude statement, Mr. Williamson. I abhor crude statements. Mind your tongue, sir. And yes, she's the one. Anyway, she moved off our senior year, remember? Everyone said she had to move off to have a baby? Well, guess what? Not only did she *not* move away to give birth to a litter of puppies, as was the rumor, but she is now a *very* successful lawyer in New York. I heard she was about to be appointed to be a judge, or something."

"Mary No-Panties a judge? You've got to be kidding me!"

"What did I say about the crude statements, mister?"

"Sorry, ma'am. Force of habit, living amongst the lower life forms in those ambulances. Some of it must have rubbed off. I will strive to do better."

"See to it that you do. Now, hand me the salad tongs, potty-mouth."

They sat down to eat, continuing to compare notes on the people that they had once known. About halfway through the meal, which was absolutely delicious as far as Byron was concerned, it struck him that he had truly missed Amber. There hadn't been a great deal of time for them to spend together while he was married to Samantha, obviously. Samantha had known about Amber's feelings for him, but had treated her with a smug, condescending attitude that bordered on contempt. Byron had also known about Amber's feelings, but she had been the one true friend he had had in his youth that was also female, and he was terrified of ruining that by attempting a relationship. He had seen it happen, and he didn't want it to happen with them. Amber had been one of the few… well, no, the *only* real friend he had ever made in Dawkin's Mills. They had been in school together since the fourth grade, and they had just clicked. Of course, that was after he had been punched in the stomach for pulling her ponytail during recess. She had one hell of a right hook for a small girl.

He grinned at the irony. In his heartfelt desire to keep Amber a part of his life, he had arranged matters so that they could not be close at all. She had always been her pleasant, upbeat self whenever their paths had crossed in the E.R., which by the nature of their jobs, was often. Byron had detected something about her after his marriage to Samantha, a slight distance, but he had never been a champion of picking up on the subtle undercurrents of human emotion, especially when that emotion came from a member of the female gender. Looking at her now, her face animated as she related a story about a boy they had known that had been caught masturbating behind the gym, he realized that he had been missing something vital to him, and he hadn't even had the sense to realize what it was.

While he was married he could be forgiven, he supposed, for that distance, but his marriage has ended over six months ago. Of course, Liza had occupied most of Byron's waking mind, and most of his dreams as well, but why was it that he was just now coming back around to one of the people that had been his anchor earlier in life? Christ, what else had he been neglecting? Well, his health, obviously, but he was working on that one. But what else?

With a start, he realized that he hadn't even spoken to Robbie since the conversation about going fishing. How many days ago had that been? Four? Five? Jesus, had he gone most of the week without speaking to his son *at all?* It was so easy to get wrapped up in just how shitty life had been treating him that he had just pretty much let everyone important to him float away in the breeze. He felt his face darken with shame. *That shit ends tonight*, he thought. *I've got two kids, not one, and they both mean the world to me. In fact, I think I'm looking at the only other person on the frigging planet that matters to me.*

Amber was still talking, and making a very obscene gesture to illustrate her point for someone that had been chiding him on his crudity earlier, when Byron reached across the table and stopped her words with a kiss. It was gentle, but the underlying current of desire was unmistakable. When their lips parted, Amber gave out a small gasp and looked at him, her eyes huge.

"Not that I'm complaining," she said, "but what brought *that* on? I'd hate to think that I need to talk about a pubescent boy's masturbation to get your motor running, but whatever works, I guess."

Byron laughed. "Sorry Amber, but hearing about Pete Brodsky's sex life, or lack thereof, doesn't really get me too hot and bothered. It's just you. I've taken you for granted for so long. Why in God's name have you put up with it? You're beautiful. You're intelligent. You're... well, you're perfect. Why have you put up with my bullshit for so long? I don't deserve you."

Amber grew completely still. After a long silence, she gave Byron the little crooked grin he had always loved best. "I love you, Byron. If you haven't figured that out by now, you really *have* done some serious damage with all that booze."

Fuck, here came the boy with Waterworks, Inc. He really wished they would take a day off every now and then. They needed to unionize, or something. Dashing his eyes with the back of his hand, he looked back at Amber. Without reason or logic, he was suddenly overcome with a lust so powerful he felt his hands shaking. He hadn't been this overwhelmed by a physical need for someone since he had been a much younger man, when he spent at least ninety percent of his life with one fantasy after another rolling through his mind, turning him into a XXX theater on legs.

Brushing his plate away from him, he stood and took the two steps that brought him to Amber's chair. His legs, which had felt like they were made of Play-Doh about four seconds earlier, now felt like he could piston them and send himself straight through the ceiling. He reached down and picked Amber up bodily and swung her towards the bedroom. Amber said, "Hey, what about dinner? It'll go to waste!"

"*Fuck* dinner," he growled at her. "I'll make you breakfast."

The next few moments were a tangle of clothing and limbs. Somehow it seemed to Byron that they never stopped kissing, even as he pulled his shirt off. Amber's breath was coming in short pants, and Byron was breathing like a dragon on steroids. They fell into the bed, touching, grasping, caressing. It seemed to him that he could not be close enough to her, could get enough *of* her. He felt as if he could crawl inside her skin and live there forever. He felt he was something just beyond a mortal man at that instant. He had *never* felt like this with Samantha, *ever*. Hell, his *ears* were ringing. He continued to kiss Amber until she pulled back long enough to pull in a tidal breath of air. Looking at him through her disheveled hair, she said, "Hadn't you better answer that?"

Byron looked at her in confusion. "*What?*"

"Your phone, silly," she said, flicking her chin at his crumpled jeans on the floor. Sure enough, the ringing he had been hearing hadn't been from simple blood loss to his brain. His phone. His god-*damn* phone. He looked at her like she had lost her mind. "You think I'm answering that fucking chatterbox son of a bitch right *now?!?*"

She laughed, and then turned sober. "You might need to. It could be the hospital. And watch your mouth," she followed up with a grin.

In a huff, Byron climbed off the bed, shooting daggers at Amber when she giggled at his bare ass. He jerked the phone out of his pocket and flipped it open.

"This is Byron, and this had better be fucking *important*!"

There was silence on the line. He was just about to tell whoever had the lousiest timing on the planet to go commit a physiologically impossible act on themselves when he heard Samantha say, "Well, yeah, I guess it is a little important, but if you're *busy*, I'll let you go."

Byron held his temper with an almost inhuman effort. "Sorry, Samantha. I thought you were someone else. What's up?"

There was more silence from the phone, and Byron took it from his ear to make sure he hadn't dropped the call. He hadn't. "Sam?"

Her voice was completely devoid of emotion. She sounded like a machine. "I just thought you would like to know that your daughter died tonight. At nine forty-eight, to be exact. If you would like to see her before they take her to the morgue, I suggest you get here soon."

There was a sterile *click*, and then dead air. Bryon stood there, his penis now not only flaccid, but seeming to try to crawl right up into his abdomen, following his already-fled balls. Dead air. No, that wasn't it. Dead daughter. Dead daughter air? No, just dead daughter. Right. Okay. Got it.

He began dressing, slowly and methodically. Underwear, right-side out: check. Socks... where were his socks? Oh, he still had them on. Right, socks: check. Pants, right leg, left leg, button zip: check. Shirt, over head, arms through: Check. No, wait, it was inside out. Turn it around. Repeat procedure. Shirt: check. Boots, over in the corner. Boots on, lacings tied: check. Someone was screaming. Who was screaming? Who was hitting him?

He looked over at Amber, over her and through her. She backed away from that awful gaze. There was nothing human in it. She began screaming again. "What? Oh, God, Byron tell me what!!! Oh, sweet Jesus, is it Liza? Tell me she isn't dead!!! Tell me she isn't dead, *please*!!!"

"She isn't dead," Byron said.

Amber fell back onto the bed, sobbing. "Damn you, you scared the shit out of me, you bastard! What happened?"

"Liza died," Byron said.

Amber cut loose with fresh wails. "You said she wasn't dead!!!"

"You told me to," Byron said.

Amber looked horrified. "What? *What???*"

"I have to go now. I have to go before they take Liza to the morgue. That's what she said. Samantha. 'If you would like to see her before they take her to the morgue, I suggest you get here soon.' That's what she said. I have to go now. Good-bye Amber. Thank you for dinner. It was very good. I like fried chicken a lot."

Byron walked out of the bedroom and through the kitchen. He picked his keys up off the washing machine and closed the door behind him softly, softening the weeping coming from the bedroom a little, but not cutting it off completely. He got into his truck and pulled out onto the road.

Chapter Twenty-Six

Byron had absolutely no recollection of the drive from Amber's house to the hospital. It was probably a good thing she lived as close as she did, or he would have most likely killed himself or someone else along the way. He now sat in the parking lot of the hospital, staring out his windshield at the bugs battering the street light. Lightening flashed, and scattered raindrops began hitting the windshield. He felt very distant from himself, almost as if he were watching himself watch the bugs.

But something was coming. Oh, yes, something was coming. He could feel it. It was like a far-off train. It would seem to be a long way off until it rounded that last curve, and then it would be *here*. Byron didn't want to be around when it got here, but he dimly realized that he didn't have a choice. He looked stupidly around the interior of his truck, wondering why he was there. Something in the back of his mind tried to inform him, but he pushed it away.

His eyes happened across the pharmacy bag he had picked up a lifetime ago, this afternoon. He hadn't even bothered to see what Franklin had prescribed him. He opened the bag and poured its contents into his lap. He lifted the bottles one by one. Standard stuff, really. Antidepressants, mostly. Oh, but what was *this?* Valium, 10 milligrams. He read the bottle. "Take one tablet by mouth twice daily," he read. Okey-dokey.

He opened the bottle and shook a half dozen of the small blue pills into his hand. That voice in the back of his mind said that probably wasn't enough. He shook out about ten more. There. That ought to help. He cast about, trying to find something to wash the pills down with, and his hand came into contact with his army canteen. *There you are, you little fucker*, he thought. He spun off the top and tossed the pills into his mouth. He took a long pull on the canteen, and nearly vomited into his lap. The orange juice had most certainly *not* improved in the hot interior of his truck. He fought a momentary battle with his stomach, until he was sure everything was going to stay down. Hell, the vodka should have kept the O.J. from going *too* bad. Then he simply sat there, his fingers trying to tap in time with the rainfall on the roof of the truck.

He had no idea how long he had sat there when he realized that he was supposed to *be* somewhere. Where was it? The hospital, right? Okay, he had that part in hand. He could see the front entrance from where he sat. But wasn't there a reason for him being at the hospital? He worked here, right? He cast about in his mind trying to find an answer until he finally just gave up and climbed out of the truck into the rain. Someone inside would know where he was supposed to be.

He walked slowly towards the entrance, liking the feeling of rain on his face. He looked upward and opened his mouth to catch some of the rain on his tongue. He was standing there like that when a voice snapped his attention towards the entrance.

"Ram? Jesus Christ, Ram, I am so fucking *sorry!*"

To Byron's bemused stare, Doctor Franklin was walking towards him with a folded newspaper held over his head. *That's not helping, Doc,* he thought. *Your hair is plastered.* This made him laugh, for some reason. A fleeting image of Franklin's hair sitting at a bar, ordering shots of tequila from a reluctant bartender shot across his mind. Franklin was right up close to him now, putting his hand on Byron's shoulder. That was all right. Byron liked Doc Franklin. He was good people. Because it seemed like something was required of him at this point, he put his hand on Franklin's shoulder too. That seemed all right.

Franklin was talking about something, but his voice was coming from a thousand miles away. Byron had to concentrate very hard to make it out.

"Ram, Samantha wanted her taken on down to the morgue, but I convinced them to wait a bit. I think you need to see her in her room, with all her stuffed animals. She looks really good, Ram. Just like she's sleeping."

"Yeah, Liza's gone asleepun."

Franklin looked confused, and then concerned.

"Ram, do you know where you are?"

Byron looked comically surprised at the question. "We're at the hospital. Sacred Heart. I work here, in the EMS department. You work here, too. Right?"

Franklin led Byron inside the doors and out of the rain. As they stood dripping, Franklin turned and looked Byron straight in the eye.

"Yes, Ram, we're at Sacred, and yes, you work here. But do you know why you're here right now?"

Byron thought very hard. "Samantha called me. She called me on the phone, but I thought it was in my ears. The ringing, I mean, not the phone. It's not a Bluetooth." This last he said as if imparting a great secret. "She called on the phone and Amber said I should answer it, but I was mad, 'cause I was naked. Well, I wasn't mad 'cause I was naked, I was mad that the phone rang *while* I was naked. You know what I mean."

Franklin nodded sagely, leading Byron over to the bank of elevators. He pushed the 3 and stood waiting beside Byron for the elevator to arrive. "Okay. Then what happened?" he asked.

Byron shrugged. "I got my clothes on and drove over here, I guess. I don't know. I took some of your pills, by the way. They help. I feel pretty good."

Franklin peered into Byron's face. "How many pills did you take, Ram? And which ones were they?"

Again Byron had to think. Thinking was getting hard, and he hoped he wouldn't have to do it much more. He liked Doc, but this was getting a little aggravating. "I took the Valium, 10 milligrams. Take one tablet by mouth twice daily." He looked proudly at Franklin. He had remembered.

"Okay, Ram," Franklin said. "How many did you take, do you know?"

Dammit, this was getting ridiculous. "If I would have known there was going to be a fucking test, I would have studied, Doc," he said with some heat.

This seemed to satisfy Franklin. The elevator binged and slid open. They stepped inside and waited for the doors to close. Once they were on their way up, Franklin looked over at Byron. His voice was calm. "Ram, do you understand that Liza died tonight? Do you understand that?"

Byron looked surprised for a moment, and then shrugged again. "Yeah, Samantha said that. She's stupid, though. She wouldn't know if Liza was dead or not. She's never had any training." To his surprise, a tear wound its way down Franklin's face.

"Oh, Ram. Oh, man, this is so *fucked*."

Byron reached out for Franklin, concerned. "Hey, are you all right, Doc? You look like shit, man. Do you need something? You want some of my pills? They help, you know."

At that moment, the elevator binged open again, and Byron glanced down the hallway. There were a large cluster of people standing around Liza's room. Too many people. He started walking down the hall. He heard Franklin calling out behind him, but paid no mind. It was coming now. The train was almost around that last corner. He began to falter in his stride. The hall seemed much longer than he remembered it. The train was almost here. Fuck, he had to hurry. He had to get to Liza's room before it got here. He tried to run, but his feet felt like they had been dipped in lead. *Nightmares*, he thought almost incoherently. *You can't run in nightmares, I don't think.*

Somehow, he made it to Liza's doorway. All these people were in his way, but he moved through them. They all had something to tell him, something to say. He couldn't hear it over the train. God, it was so *close*. He entered the room and saw Samantha sitting in the chair next to Liza's bed. She was weeping in a soft way, like a slow leak. Byron's eyes traveled up the bed to Liza's still form. She lay on her side, one arm draped over her favorite bear. Her eyes were closed, and she did look asleep, at least until his eyes, his damned *trained* eyes reported to his brain the death they saw. He tried to close them, but they remained stubbornly open. He opened his mouth, but couldn't speak. His tongue was super glued to the roof of his mouth. With a monumental effort, he wrenched it loose. "Liza?" he heard himself say…

The train arrived.

Chapter Twenty-Seven

The rest of that evening had been a carnival ride of horror. Byron was utterly unable to function, emotionally or physically.

Franklin had threatened to have his stomach pumped if he didn't pull it together. After the orderlies had taken Liza down to the morgue, Byron had been forcibly put in bed by Franklin. He wouldn't give Byron anything to help him sleep, fearing what the reaction to the Valium would be.

As it turned out, there was no need. Byron was out like a light within moments of lying down on the couch in Franklin's office. He vaguely remembered laughing at that. When Franklin asked him what was funny, Byron had replied that he had people trying to get him on a psychiatrist's couch for years. Franklin had just smiled, and told Byron to get some sleep.

"Do not get off that couch until I come and get you, do you read me?" Franklin had asked.

"Nous Resterons La", Byron had replied sleepily.

Franklin looked confused. "What?"

Byron said it again. "'Nous Resterons La'. It's the motto of my unit. 3rd Infantry. It means 'We Will Stay Here'. Maybe since it's just me, I should use the first-person singular. That would be 'Je vais rester ici', I think. Je n'ai pas parlé français pendant un certain temps, so I'm not sure. "

Franklin stood quietly for a moment. "Ram, just out of curiosity, how many languages do you speak?" Byron thought about it laboriously for several minutes and finally said, "Well, let's see. English, of course. Then there's French, German and Arabic. Oh, and some regular Latin and *really* good Pig Latin." He laughed drowsily. "I wouldn't trust my Latin too well, though. Conjugating those verbs are a *bitch*." With that, Byron's eyes slipped closed and he fell asleep. Franklin continued to stare at Byron for a moment, mumbled "Remarkable man", and then shook his head. He turned and walked out of the room, continuing to mumble under his breath.

The next morning, Byron had awakened with no idea where the hell he was. He looked groggily around, trying to get his bearings. He swung his legs off the couch and sat up. He sat there for several moments with his head in his hands, trying to come to grips with what was going on. When it hit him, the fact that Liza was dead, he began to weep uncontrollably. He sat there shaking and weeping for the better part of an hour. Once he had some semblance of control, he had gone out of the office and down to the cafeteria. He ordered a coffee and sat at a back table drinking it alone, until Franklin had come in, looking harried. He saw Byron and walked over to his table and sat down.

"There you are, Ram. You had me kinda worried there for a second, bro."

Byron nodded. "Sorry. I woke up and had to kind of get my head together. I thought a cup of coffee might help."

"I'm sure it will. Now, a question: How much Valium did you take last night, and where is the rest of it? I'm not in the habit of helping people commit suicide, Ram." His voice was stern, but his eyes brimmed with compassion.

Byron shrugged. "I really don't know how many I took. Too many, that much is obvious. I superseded the dosage by a considerable amount, I'm sure of that. Insofar as to where the rest of it is, I figure it's laying in the seat of my truck, unless someone saw it and helped themselves to it. I honestly don't know, Doc."

Franklin rose. "Well, come on. Take your coffee to go, and let's go to your truck and see what the damage is."

They walked out into the overcast late morning together. Once at Byron's truck, they were both amazed to find to that the bottles of medicine were sitting right where he had left them.

Byron looked over at Franklin. "Well, chalk one up for the honesty of the human race, Doc. I would have never believed it."

They laughed. Franklin poured the remaining contents of the Valium into his hand and counted them back into the bottle. He looked up at Byron and shook his head.

"You seem to have taken sixteen ten-milligram Valium, and chased them down with some liquor, judging from your breath last night. So, 160 milligrams of Valium with a vodka chaser. No wonder you were all spaghetti-legged last night. I was afraid I might have had to hit you with some Anexate to counter the effects of the Valium. It's hard to overdose on that shit, but when you add booze to the mix, it can happen. Hell, you know that. You've probably dealt with more people overdosing on Valium and booze than I have. You didn't take enough to hurt you, though." He cut his eyes to Byron. "Which is really lucky for *both* of us, Ram."

Byron looked down in shame. "Doc, I'm sorry. Really. I wouldn't have done it if I had been right in the head. If you want to hold on to the rest of them, I understand."

"Ram, look at me."

Byron looked up into Franklin's eyes. He found it amazingly hard to do. This man's opinion was important to him, he realized with some surprise.

"Do you think you can keep from eating these things like Pez?" asked Franklin.

"Yeah, I can. I know what's what. Like I said, I just wasn't right in the head last night."

Franklin thought it over for a minute, and then nodded. He handed to bottle back to Byron. "Then take these. You're probably going to need them in the next few days. But take them, *correctly*. I hear you've taken too many of these puppies again, and I'll have you slapped into the psych unit for a 72 hour observation. I shit you not. You read me?"

"Five-by, Doc. No more than prescribed. Gotcha."

Franklin started to clap Byron on the shoulder, and then surprised him by hugging him tightly for a moment. Byron found himself hugging back just as hard.

When they parted, both of them were abashed to find their eyes watering.

Byron grinned. "Well, if Rutherford saw that, it'll be all over the hospital by lunch that you and I are queer for each other."

Franklin laughed. "Well, let him try. If he does, *I'll* start a rumor that he was in my office last week, telling me about his sexual fantasies about his mother."

They both broke up laughing. As the laughter tapered off, they looked at each other soberly.

"Are you ready for this, Ram?"

"Fuck, *no*, I'm not ready for this. How can you be ready for something like this? My little girl is dead, Doc. She's fucking dead, and I wasn't there for it. I was busy trying to get lu-lu-*laid*, goddamit!" Byron began weeping again, the force of it nearly taking his legs out from under him. Franklin grabbed him under the arm, and the two of them stood in the freshening rain until the worst of the pain had passed through Byron.

Once he was able, Byron had gone back into the hospital. He went to see if there was any paperwork that needed to be filled out concerning Liza and was shocked to find that Samantha had already done it. That was unlike her. She usually left everything official for Byron to take care of. Shaking his head, he left the hospital and headed for the funeral home to make the necessary arrangements.

When he arrived, he was again shocked to find that Samantha had already taken care of all *that*, too. What the hell had gotten into the woman? Did it take the death of one of her children to get her motivated? It was an unkind thought, but at the moment, Byron couldn't make himself give a damn.

He left the funeral home and returned to Amber's house. She was sitting on the couch when he came in with her legs tucked under her, staring blankly at one of the mindless day-time talk shows on TV. She turned to look at him when he came in, her eyes puffy and red from a sleepless night of weeping.

He sat next to her. Neither of them spoke for a long time. Finally, Byron broke the silence. "Amber, I am so sorry for running out of here and leaving you like that last night. I shouldn't have done that. I am really sorry."

Amber looked at him in disbelief. "You're *apologizing?* To *me?* Byron… baby… Liza *died* last night. You have absolutely nothing to apologize to me about, ever. I came to the hospital to find you, but Doctor Franklin said you were pretty zoned out, and that he had put you on his couch to sleep. I looked in on you, and then came on home. I figured I should be here in case you needed someplace to go."

She put her arms around him, and they sat like that quietly for several moments. The enormity of what had happened suddenly crashed into Byron like a physical blow.

"Amber, she's gone, isn't she?"

"Yes, baby, she is. I'm so sorry."

All the weeping he had done to this point had apparently just been warm-up for the big game. He completely lost control now, crying so hard that he slid off the couch into the floor. Amber went with him, never releasing him from her embrace. Byron wailed until it felt like his throat was about to rupture. His eyes throbbed, and his ears seemed to fill with fluid. And still he wailed. Banshees would have fled in terror at the sound coming from this man, from his soul.

She was gone. His baby was gone, forever, no take-backs. She would never talk to him again, never hug his neck. She would never watch Teletubbies again. There would be no Prom, no High School graduation, no wedding, no grandchildren, no *nothing*. She was *gone*. *Forever*.

Byron could not stand the pain of this horrid truth. In self-defense, his mind shut down, as it had in the past. He lay on Amber's living room floor like a dead man himself. The tears had stopped, and his breath had evened out. He just lay there, inert. Amber became concerned at first, but then, as she had always done in the past, she understood.

And still, she held him.

Chapter Twenty-Eight

The funeral was an exercise in emotional stamina that Byron would have never believed possible. He wasn't having one, period. *To hell with this. Why do people do this to themselves?*, he wondered. Everyone had dressed in their Sunday best and gathered around a box containing the dead body of a child. It was laughable in a terror-inducing way. How many times did he tell someone "Thank you" today when they had offered their condolences? He's lost count. And they all said the exact same shit. "She's with the angels now." "Her pain is over now." "She was young, far too young." *Well, no shit. Just shy of her fourth birthday, yeah folks, that is just a little too fucking young. But, hey, thanks for reminding me about every three minutes my little girl is dead! I'd almost forgotten there for a second!*

Byron shook his head. Maybe they should come up with a card that said all that shit, and then left a long space for everyone to sign it, thereby eliminating the need to vocalize it over and over. Probably not. No, everyone has to put in their own two cents. Just so it's, you know, *personal.*

Byron had sat in the parlor for as long as he could manage it. Which was about fifteen minutes this time. He was doing better. This was a record. Maybe by the time they got around to the actual funeral, he'd be able to sit through the whole thing. He hoped so. He got up and wandered off through the funeral home, trying to find the exit. He wished he smoked. Maybe he would start. That was where everyone that smoked congregated. They seemed to be less apt to start spouting platitudes at him out there. Maybe they were just too busy smoking.

For whatever reason, he liked it out there by the exit far better than downstairs in the dining area. It looked like some sort of church luncheon down there, with the long tables covered with dishes and platters of food that people had brought with them. Was being at a funeral supposed to make people hungry? The women were mostly grouped up down there, and he'd figured out quickly to steer clear of women, *especially* in groups. They would drive him utterly insane in about fifteen seconds with their hugs, pats, and comforting words. He didn't *want* to be comforted. He had no business being comforted right now. His little girl was lying in a box upstairs, so no, don't hand him another plate of finger sandwiches that he would just as soon shove up their asses and tell him how "This, too, shall pass", you stupid bitches. Jesus.

He made it out of the exit, but there weren't any smokers there at the present. That was okay, too. The only place he liked better than being out here near the exit with the smokers was to be out here near the exit by himself. The rain had held off for the time being, but it looked like it was ready to open up and pour at any second. He didn't mind that, either. The sky should cry, too. That seemed fitting to him.

He stood leaning up against one of the exit pillars (why the fuck did they feel the need to put Ionic columns by the *exit*, anyway?) and looked around. To his surprise, he saw Robbie standing over by his mother's car, kicking rocks around the parking lot. Byron hadn't spoken with Robbie since Liza had died. He had tried to coax him to the phone once, but Samantha had told him that Robbie was too upset to come to the phone. Well, once again, no shit. His little sister was dead. That sort of thing was likely to put a kid in a kind of upset frame of mind. Byron headed over to talk to him, glad for a chance to talk to his son without Samantha hovering around, waiting to pounce on him like a leopard on a gazelle with a gimp knee.

"Hey, Big Guy, how ya doing?" Byron asked when he got close. Robbie's head whipped around and Byron was stopped cold by the hatred he saw in his son's eyes. Robbie turned away and began to head back to the funeral home. Byron took several running steps and caught up with him.

"Robbie, what's wrong? I'm so sorry about Liza, Big Guy," he said. *Dammit, I'm starting to sound like the Greek chorus in the dining room,* he thought. He reached out and put his arm around Robbie's shoulders and was shocked at the force behind the way Robbie flung his arm away.

"Don't you talk to me. I *hate* you," Robbie his voice an icy tundra.

Byron was stupefied. "Robbie, please, what is it? What's wrong? What did *I* do?" He could hear the pleading tone of his voice, but was powerless to stop it. "Why are you mad at me? I tried to talk to you the other night on the phone, but your Mom said you didn't want to talk."

Byron had never even imagined that the eyes of a seven year old boy could hold such contempt.

"Who cares if you wanted to talk to me?" the boy snapped. "You don't love me, you don't love *nobody*, so who cares if you want to talk?"

Byron felt a cold ball form in his stomach. "Robbie, did your Mom tell you that?"

"No! *I* told me that! I'm not *stupid*, you know!" The boy was now crying, hot tears rolling unheeded down his cheeks.

"I know you're not stupid, Bobbster. You're very smart, and I do love you. I love you very much."

"Like you loved Liza?"

Oh, Jesus. "Yes, Robbie, like I loved Liza. I loved you both the same. It may not have seemed like it because I spent so much time with Liza, but that was because she was sick. Do you understand? I loved you both the same, always."

"Well, if you love me like you love Liza, then you can just *keep* your stupid old love, 'cause I don't want none!"

"What in the hell? Robbie, what are you talking about?"

The boy, now weeping so hard that he had a hard time speaking clearly, said, "You save people. That's your j-j-job! You save p-people! You save everybody, but you d-d-didn't s-save Liza, and *I HATE YOU!!!*"

Robbie tore off across the parking lot and into the funeral home. Byron knew he should go after him, but he didn't. How could he? The boy was right. It was Byron's job to save people. It was what he did. So, why hadn't he saved his little girl?

The sky finally opened up and a torrent of rain began to fall. Byron was soaked instantly, his suit clinging to his shoulders. He walked toward the funeral home, his head hung low.

Why hadn't he saved his little girl?

Chapter Twenty-Nine

The day of the funeral dawned with the sun spiking through the clouds. A brisk wind had come up, and it appeared that the rain that had been forecast might blow off to the east. Byron had been spending the nights with Amber, and he woke that morning to the soft sound of her breathing. *I'm going to bury my little girl today*, he thought. Somehow, it still didn't seem like any of this could be happening.

He slid out of bed and left the bedroom quietly. He stood in the kitchen and turned on the coffee pot. While the coffee was being made, he stared blankly out the kitchen window, watching the sun fight through the clouds. The coffee pot beeped to let him know it was done, and he went into the bathroom and opened the medicine cabinet. He shook out two of the Valium and padded back into the kitchen. He took them with a cup of coffee. He had hedged his bets somewhat with Franklin. While there had been no repeats of the massive dosage that first night, he had been taking the Valium twice a day, but doubling the dosage. It seemed to be just enough to keep the raw panic that always seemed to be clawing at the edge of his mind like a yammering, screeching animal at bay. He felt ashamed for having lied to Franklin, but he figured that if he had to face today, he was going to need every edge he could get.

He walked to the bedroom door and stood watching Amber sleep. They slept in the same bed, but sleeping was all that they did. He could not imagine attempting anything sexual, and she seemed to understand that completely. They just held each other in the darkness, and when he would weep in the dead of the night, she was there to hold him closer until it passed.

A surge of anger ran through him. It was unfair. Well, of course it was. But he was getting *better*, dammit! He was off the booze, and had found someone that loved him completely. They could build a life together. He could get back to work, and the kids would have had a home to come visit him in a *home*, not just a trailer that held his belongings. He imagined him and Amber sitting on the couch while the kids played a video game and fought good-naturedly about who was whipping who. He saw Amber there to provide Liza with the kind of professional help that Samantha just wasn't qualified to give. They could have been a family.

Now, all that was gone. Sure, he and Amber could still create a life together, but the chance of a family? No way. Not now, anyway. His baby girl was dead and his son hated his guts. Byron guessed that time might take away some of the hatred and rage that Robbie felt for him right now, but he couldn't be sure of that. It was just so god-damned *unfair!*

He bit into his fist to keep the scream that wanted to burst out locked behind his lips. Waking Amber like that would scare her badly, and he had hurt enough of the people he loved. Robbie's accusation still burned in his heart. His logical mind knew that he was a paramedic, not a pediatric oncologist, but logic and love were at best very distant cousins, and they never even said hello to one another at the family reunions. *Why?*, he asked God, or Whoever was in charge. *Why my baby? Why those girls in Fallujah? You have a hard-on for offing little girls, you prick?*

Of course, he got no answer. Not that he expected one. He walked into the bedroom and turned off the alarm clock just before it was about to go off at seven. He'd wake Amber up in a little bit. She was looking as drawn and tired as he felt. She could use a little more sleep. He went back into the bathroom and turned on the shower. Lathering up, he shaved while in the shower, something he had picked up in the Army and had never let go of. It was a time saver. If you were going to be a life saver, you needed to know lots of time savers. That thought set him off again, and he wept in the shower. He was amazed he wasn't dehydrated from shedding so many tears lately. There was little possibility of an eye infection with him, as well-irrigated as he was keeping his eyes.

By the time he stepped out of the shower, he felt calmer, more in control. He assumed the Valium was beginning to kick in and do its job. *God bless whoever invented that shit,* he thought, before remembering that he wasn't on particularly good terms with God, if He even existed. He brushed he teeth and checked himself in the mirror. The man looking back wasn't the picture of emotional health and well-being, but he would do. He would have to.

Today wasn't about Liza, he had realized. Funerals never really are. The dead don't care. Funerals were a way for the living to accept that part of their lives was forever gone. Byron didn't want to accept that, but there it was. No, today was about the living, and no matter how his son felt towards him right now, Robbie was going to need all the support he could get. So would Samantha, he supposed, not that she would accept any from him. If he could make it through the day without Samantha slapping him, he would count it as a victory.

Not that she had done anything like that so far. She had avoided him studiously up to this point, and on the rare occasions that they had been forced into brief conversation, she had been distantly contempt toward him. That was fine by him. At least there was no chance of having Robbie see his mother beating the shit out of his father that way. Of course, Robbie might well enjoy that right now, may even want to join in. Byron cursed, spat into the basin, and walked back into the bedroom.

The bed was empty, but neatly made. It still amazed him how organized Amber was. "Everything in its place" seemed to be her motto. In his trailer, the bed had never even had the sheets washed, let alone made. He shook his head and went into the kitchen.

Amber was sitting at the small breakfast nook, drinking a cup of coffee. She smiled sadly up at him as he walked in.

"You turned the alarm off. How long have you been up?"

"Not long. I just thought you could use a little more sleep, that's all. I went ahead and got my shower out of the way. How are you this morning?"

She sighed. "I'm not ready for today. I don't want to do this. And if I feel this badly, I can't even begin to imagine how you're feeling. But that's so like you, Byron. We're sitting here on the morning of your daughter's funeral, and you still think to let me get some more sleep, make the coffee, and ask me how *I* am this morning. You are a beautiful man, and I love you."

Byron had always felt uncomfortable when someone had given him a compliment of any kind. It was just hard-wired into his genetic make-up, he supposed. But coming from Amber, all he could feel was gratitude. She meant it. For reasons he would never understand, she really loved him.

"I love you, too, Amber. I never really thought that I would say that to another woman again, but I do. I just wish that we had done this months ago. This is no way to start a relationship."

"I know," she said sadly, "but it's better now than if we had never done it at all." She stood up and poured the remainder of her coffee down the sink. "I'm going to get in the shower. Your suit is hanging on the back of the closet door. I wasn't sure what tie you would want, so I laid out all three of them."

They had gone together the evening before to the local men's store and she had helped him pick out a new suit. The only one he owned was old and looked a little tattered around the edges, she had told him. He could tell by the way she had hesitated in picking out the words that what she really meant was that the suit looked like something a hobo might wear at dinner at a 5-star Dumpster. Byron realized that, not counting his dress uniform in the Army, the only other times in his life he had worn a suit were at funerals and weddings. *Well, today is no exception*, he thought. This one would be worn today, and then hung in the back of the closet to await the next celebration, be it of love or death. Sometimes they were celebrations of the same thing.

He took the suit off the rack and began dressing himself. Amber had draped his three ties across a hanger. He stood staring at them, unable to decide which one to put one. He was alarmed to find Amber coming out of the bathroom, her hair up in a towel. He glanced at the clock and was shocked to see that he had been standing there looking at the ties for almost a half an hour. *Pull it together, Sergeant*, he told himself in his toughest tone. He reached out decisively and took the last tie on the rack. Made of silk, it was black with thin gold striped running diagonally down it. Amber smiled at him and nodded her chin toward the tie in his hand.

"I'm glad you picked that one. It's the prettiest of the three. You've got a good eye for that."

Byron smothered a crazed laugh. Should he tell her that he had picked it blindly, after staring at the fucking things for a half hour? No, that was probably not the best idea at the moment. He just nodded instead and proceeded to knot the thing around his neck. *Why do we even wear these things,* he wondered. *It's like we're tying a noose around our necks and then proudly displaying it to the world. Here I am, choke me!*

They finished getting ready and headed out to the funeral parlor. The funeral wasn't until eleven-thirty, but he felt that he needed to be there as early as possible. There was a clock in his head, rapidly counting backwards until that moment when he would no longer see Liza's face again. That was the moment that frightened him the most. The grave side service didn't bother him as much, because in his mind, they would just be burying a box. He had been to enough military funerals to understand that. That box could have *anything* in it. It was closed. But when they were finished with the service at the funeral home, they would lower the lid on the coffin, and Byron would never look at his little girl again. *That* was what he dreaded, and *that* was what that damned clock was rapidly counting down to.

He did all right in the funeral parking lot, and did all right again at the entrance. He even did all right as he made his way down the hall. But once he reached the parlor that held Liza, he seized up. Utterly and completely seized up. His legs refused to move, and his lungs had stopped working. He gave out a strangled little gasp and Amber pulled him back to one of the small couches in the hallway and sat him down. He looked at her with dumb gratitude. If she hadn't been there to pull him back, he was pretty sure he would have died there in that parlor door of asphyxia.

He sat on the hallway couch until he felt he was better in control of himself. With shaky legs, he rose and went back to the parlor door. He hesitated at the threshold and then, steeling his resolve, he stepped into the room. If he had vapor-locked at that instant and dropped dead to the floor, he would have counted himself a lucky man, because then Liza wouldn't go into the dark alone. He forced himself to move forward, one step at time, until he stood beside the casket.

It was so pitifully small, and once again, Byron was overwhelmed by a surge of rage that left his hands shaking. *What kind of goddamn world do we live in where there is even a* need *for a coffin this fucking small?* he wondered. He slowly brought his eyes up the coffin until they rested on Liza's peaceful face. She looked like she was ready to jump into his arms and have him give her a piggy-back ride around the room. *She looks healthier in death than she did while she was alive. How is that possible, and why does it make me so damned mad?*

He stood there for a long time, taking in every detail. It was quite a while before he could work up the courage to touch her. He had touched death hundreds, if not thousands of times, in his life but he was hesitant to do so now. This wasn't a nameless car wreck victim or an overdose, a run sheet to fill out and move on to the next run. This wasn't some unlucky soldier who zigged when he should have zagged and caught a stray round in the throat. This was is baby *daughter* lying here. His hand hung in midair just above Liza's face, wavering.

"Go ahead," spoke a voice at his side. "Touch her. You need this, to do this. You will regret it forever if you let them close that coffin without touching Liza at least once more."

Byron had uttered a tiny *eep!* at this unexpected voice, and turned to find Amber standing at his side. With her little chin-nod, she motioned for him to go on. She took his free hand in hers and held it tightly; giving him all the strength she could muster.

Byron looked at the hand that hovered there undecided, it hit him how many times that same hand had saved a life, or taken one. He was amazed at the irony of that simple appendage. It was so easy to end a human life, sometimes with something as simple as applying three pounds of pressure on a trigger. But it was equally difficult to save that human life after that trigger had been pulled. His hand, hovering, savior, killer… what was the difference anymore?

He ground his teeth and forced himself to lower that hand onto Liza's too-still cheek. As he had feared, the flesh had lost that vital spark that is instantly recognizable between life and death. One minute, a lifetime of possibility, a second later, only so much meat on a slab, all promise ended.

He stroked her face, and moved her hair slightly out of her eyes. The treatments had caused it to fall out, but it had grown back black and baby-fine. He moved his hand about her face, exploring those hidden climes that only a parent can ever know about their children. This tiny scar, the time she hit her head on the coffee table learning to walk. How it had bled, Samantha shrieking that Liza was going to bleed to death even after Byron had already staunched the flow. This slightly higher eyebrow, giving that side of her face a questioning look at all times. All these landmarks, soon to be buried under six feet of cold earth.

Byron was weeping again, although he didn't know it. He leaned down and kissed Liza on that still-soft spot between her eyebrows. This had always elicited a smile from her, no matter what her mood. Not this time, or ever again. That smile was gone. Byron stood back and looked down at his daughter. Amber was wiping his fallen tears from Liza's cheek. Without a word, Byron turned on his heel and left the room.

He barely found the bathroom before he vomited until it felt as if his stomach was actually going to climb out of his throat and fall into the basin. He stood at the mirror, wiping his mouth as he stared into his eyes. Nothing there but rage. He fumbled open the Valium and took several more. *Fuck* Doctor Franklin. His little girl wasn't laying in a box a few rooms away waiting to be stuck in the ground like a flower that would never grow.

He sat down on the commode, his head in his hands. For no reason at all, he found himself thinking of Specialist Kevin MacDonald. Those days at the FOB were hazy, some of it drugs, some of it just him, he supposed. As he waited for the Valium to begin to do its thing, he membered the last time he had seen Specialist Kevin MacDonald.

Chapter Thirty

Byron jerked awake unaware of his surroundings. He was in a military installation; that much was immediately clear from the number of uniforms he saw walking around. But where, and why? Had he been hit in the ambush? He ran his hands up and down his body, feeling for wounds. He found nothing. The last clear memory he had was of the rounds whizzing around the column, and of a group of civilians being caught in the crossfire. Some of them had been children, hadn't they? Little girls, all alike? It seemed that they had been. He shook his head and tried to rise from his bed. He was immediately rewarded with a spinning head that physically dropped him back onto the mattress.

Had he been drugged? It felt like it. Everything around him held a gauzy film around it, giving lights a nimbus halo. When someone passed by, it seemed they left a contrail of light behind them. Something was definitely *not* normal here. He lay back and tried to get his bearings.

He was still working through why he was in a hospital when McDonald walked up. Byron had successfully managed to ascertain that he was, in fact, in a hospital, but was still stuck on why.

"Hey Sarge, how you feelin'?" asked McDonald.

"I dunno. Whash happen'? Why'm I inna hoshpital?" slurred Byron. "Did I get hit inna head?"

"No, Sarge, you're fine. No holes other than those you came equipped with. You feeling all right? Your eyes look a little weird."

"Sumbody drugged me, I think," Byron answered. "Issar any wa'er? I'm so thirsty."

McDonald reached over to the table beside Byron's bed and picked up a plastic pitcher and glass. He poured a glassful for Byron, who drained it at one go. He held the glass out. "More?"

McDonald refilled his glass. This time, Byron took his time, sipping the water to re-hydrate his swollen-feeling tongue. After he had drunk all his water, he spoke slightly more clearly.

"Kevin, what in the hell is going on? I'm not hurt, but I'm in a medical center. That makes zero sense. Plus, I feel like I'm on acid, or something. Your face keeps rearranging itself, for one thing. Your eyes and your mouth change places, and it's disturbing. I wish you'd stop it."

McDonald smiled. "Sorry about that, Sarge. I'll work on it." His face grew somber. "Do you really not know why you're here?

Byron shook his head. "The last thing I remember is the ambush. I could hear the rounds impacting the vehicles. And then, I remember some civilians getting wounded. I was on my way to tend them, next thing I know, I wake up here. Although…" He paused, his brow furrowed in thought. "Didn't one of our guys get hit? It seems like we took a KIA. It was... Henderson, wasn't it?"

He looked at McDonald in confusion. McDonald nodded.

"That's right, Sarge. Henderson was the only KIA in the convoy." McDonald looked uncomfortable. Byron raised his eyes for an explanation. McDonald cleared his throat and began to pluck at the seams of his ACU pants nervously.

Byron finally lost his patience. He looked at McDonald and said, "Specialist, do I need to order you to tell me what's going on, or what?"

McDonald looked at Byron with conflict in his eyes. "Sarge, are you being straight with me? No bullshit? You've got no idea what happened on that convoy?"

"Goddammit, McDonald, how many times do I need to tell you that? I'm not being by-God debriefed by a *Specialist*, am I?" Byron's voice dripped sarcasm.

McDonald's eyes took on a hard glint. He snapped to attention, and stood perfectly ram-rod straight. When he answered, it was in a military monotone, as if he were making a report to a superior. McDonald kept his eyes looking into the middle distance over Byron's left shoulder.

"Sergeant, on the day in question, the convoy did, in fact, come under ambush attack by retreating assailants, identity of which unknown. Small arms fire was exchanged. No one in the convoy was hit by this. The enemy was merely giving us harassment fire, in order to slow us down as they made their way through the city. The volume of fire dropped, and it appeared for all intents and purposes that the firefight was coming to an end. Private Henderson was screaming for a target throughout the exchange. Since he could find none, he turned his .50 on the non-combatants taking cover on the corner. He wounded several and killed three before he was KIA himself. You treated the dead and wounded, and were medevac'd here."

Byron looked at McDonald in confusion. "If the firefight had ended, how did Henderson get popped?"

McDonald never lost his rigid military bearing. "Private Henderson's death has been ruled a friendly-fire fratricide, Sergeant."

"Well, who fired, and why wasn't I informed? I could have possibly saved his fucking life, you know. It's what I do."

McDonald's eyes grew softer. "No, Sergeant, I don't think you could have saved him. He was killed instantly."

Byron's voice shook with rage. "As the medic on that convoy, it's *my* decision who is dead and who is not, Specialist."

McDonald finally looked back into Byron's eyes. When he spoke, his voice was so soft that Byron could barely make it out.

"No, Sergeant, not this time. You did too good a job of killing Henderson for him to have any chance of survival."

Byron was beyond words. He gaped at McDonald for a full minute before he could squeak out the words. *"What did you say?"*

McDonald reached out and took Byron's limp hand and held it tightly in his own.

"Sarge, Henderson was massacring those civilians. Civilian *kids*. You did the best thing you could. You've been here for three days since it happened. They've kept you pretty medicated, but pretty soon, the brass is going to want to debrief you. May be over-stepping myself here, but maybe *not* remembering what happened after we came under fire might be the best thing."

Byron was still all at sea. "Are you telling me that *I* killed Henderson? That I actually *killed* one of my own men? Is that what you're telling me?"

McDonald shook his head. "It was none of my business to tell you anything about any of this shit. They've had me bird-dogging you since we got here. I've been... well, I guess I've been a combination of moral support and a guard." He nodded at his rifle, slung over the back of his chair. "I don't know why they figure me for a guard," he continued, "At least as far as you're concerned. If it was up to me, you could waltz right out of here if you wanted. In my eyes, you did what you had to do. If you had charged out to those civilians, Henderson would have cut you in half. You ended that threat before you moved into a new sector. Isn't that what we're trained to do?"

Byron lay back on his bed, staring unseeingly at the ceiling. The first time he tried to speak, his voice was a strangled croak. McDonald poured him some more water, and Byron drained it again. His second attempt was better.

"How did I kill him?" he asked quietly.

"You fired four times up under his body armor. From the angle you fired, the rounds passed under the armor and exited through his head, face, and throat. Believe me, Sarge; he was dead before he hit the floor of the Humvee."

Byron laid totally still, his mind numb. "How can I not remember doing that?" he asked.

"You were kinda… well, you were sorta fucked up at the time, Sarge," McDonald replied. "You spent the better part of a half hour trying to reassemble those kids, for the love of God on His throne! I was nearly sick as a dog watching you. You worked your ass off for those kids, Sarge, I swear you did."

"Wait… something… yeah, the pediatric intensive care facility, I remember that. Someone said the kids were being taken to…" His words faded and he gave McDonald a haunted look. "No such thing, is there? I fucking *knew* that. Oh, God." Byron shed the first of a great many tears to come.

McDonald held his hand even harder. "Sarge, the brass are calling this friendly-fire. Let's let them keep that up, what do you say? I mean, if you have any more sudden recollections, why don't you just keep them to yourself?"

Byron turned his head away from McDonald, and would speak no more, no matter what was said to him. For Sergeant Byron Williamson, the war in Iraq was over. After a brief session with a Major, who asked only desultory questions, the whole affair was written off as a tragic accident. Fog of war, and all that. Fratricide was a horrible thing, but such things occurred when human beings fired weapons at or around each other in anger. Private Henderson was to be given a military funeral with full honors, Byron was told. For the first time since that day on the convoy, Bryon had found himself laughing. The Major gave Byron a long look, then shook his head. When he spoke again, his voice was clipped and precise. "Sergeant Williamson, from the after-report I've read from Captain Leonard and First Sergeant Fleming, your actions saved the lives of several civilians, and that you rushed to the aid of those civilians with no thought to your own safety. Your bravery was apparent in your actions. While both Captain Leonard and First Sergeant Fleming feel you deserve a medal for your actions, I'm afraid that due to the unfortunate fatality of Private Henderson, it could be viewed as somewhat... *inappropriate* to award you a medal at this time. I'm sure you understand, Sergeant."

Byron simply nodded and snapped a salute back at the Major as he was leaving. A medal? Did the U.S. Army even *have* a medal for killing one of your own?

Byron was sent stateside to finish his enlistment. He was not approached to reenlist. He finished his time in the Army at Fort Stewart, Georgia, working at the base hospital. He left the Army and went straight home, to his small Tennessee town, where he hoped to forever shed the sands of Iraq from his body, mind, and soul.

But as anyone that has ever been to the beach can tell you, sand is almost impossible to get completely off; you are forever finding errant grains much later when you least expect them.

Chapter Thirty-One

Byron was able to make it through the funeral much better than he would have ever imagined. Whether it was the Valium or that he was simply dry of emotional recoil, he found himself sitting in the front pew looking at Liza as the pastor droned on about how we, as mere humans, could not begin to understand God's great plan for us all, but he was sure that God had placed Liza on this earth for a reason, and that all that knew her were enriched by that association. *Sure, fucktard,* Byron thought, *you never even met her. How would you know? She could have been an angel on earth, or a complete hellion. All you want to do is get this over so you can catch the game on TV, so let's get this show on the road.*

Across the aisle, Samantha and Robbie sat, tears rolling steadily down both their faces. Outwardly, Byron showed nothing. No tears, no expression. He could have been carved of oak, so stark and unchanging was his face. Only Amber seemed to understand, and even when his grip became so tight it was painful, she held on to him.

After the obligatory harangue about life eternal and how one had to prepare to meet thy God Almighty, there was a truly vile version of Amazing Grace sung by a woman that was completely off-key and fish-eyed to boot. Byron wasn't sure if he had ever heard such a horrid thing before in his life. Once the woman was finished torturing any dog within a mile radius of the funeral home, the mourners began to file out.

The clock in Byron's head that had been steadily counting down was now in the red. There were only moments left, only seconds. He felt a momentary surge of panic, and then the cold emptiness filled him again. He stood and looked on as Samantha and Robbie said their final goodbyes to Liza. Samantha kissed Liza's cold cheek, and Robbie placed her favorite stuffed bear next to her on the satin lined pillow. Samantha gave a wail of grief at this and pulled Robbie into a tight embrace. They stayed that way for several moments. Byron knew his place in this scene, forever on the outside, never to be allowed into this circle of love. He and Robbie might one day have had a relationship of sorts, but their unquestioning love was gone, as dead as Liza herself. Still, Byron could not bring himself to go to them.

As Samantha and Robbie turned to leave, Samantha gave Byron a look so scathing and full of hatred that he almost took an involuntary step backward. There was nothing short of his death in her eyes. As she walked passed him, she spoke in a low, furious tone.

"Never again do you call my home. Not for any reason. If you want to see Robbie, find a good lawyer. He wants nothing to do with you. You may want to take that into consideration if you *do* hire a lawyer. Judges don't make kids his age visit their parents if they don't want to. It creates a "run-away" situation. I've done some research. So, call my house one time, try to see Robbie at school or anywhere else, and I'll have you in jail so goddamn fast *your* head will spin. Got that, *hero?*"

Amber gasped. "Samantha, Sammy, please…"

Samantha's head whipped around like a striking viper. "Shut your mouth, bitch. The same goes for you. You want him? You've got him. Fuck him silly until he breaks your heart. Best of luck."

With that, she spun on her heel and walked out of the funeral parlor, Robbie in tow.

Neither of them looked back.

"Oh, Byron, I am so sorry that happened. Just give it time, she'll come around, you'll see…"

Byron silenced Amber with a finger to her lips.

"I've only got a few more seconds to see my little girl. I'm just going to do that, okay? I'll worry about everything else later. Okay? Why don't you say your goodbye to Liza first?" He gestured to the open coffin.

Amber looked hesitant, but moved to the coffin and touched Liza's face, just once. Her voice was pitched very low, but Byron heard her quite well.

"Be at peace, little one. No more pain. Love you, Liza-Bug."

Byron was growing closer and closer to the panic that had been in the recesses of his mind, just beyond that cold void that has been so helpful during the service. That clock was moving far too fast. Amber walked a distance away and stood waiting for Byron to finish this final task.

Byron walked up to the casket and laid his hands on the satin lining. He stood looking down at what remained of his daughter. Finally, he leaned over and kissed Liza between the eyebrows and whispered into her ear.

"If you're still close enough to hear me, baby girl, this is Daddy. I'll see you soon. I promise. I'll see you soon, and we'll catch the biggest fish you ever saw. You just wait. Daddy loves you, Liza."

With that, he turned away. The clock in his mind reached a flashing set of red zeroes. He had only taken a few steps when he looked back. As he expected, the men behind the coffin had already closed the coffin and were removing the flowers from around it so they could move it to the hearse. Just agents of death, going about their business. Just one more link in the chain that Byron himself had been a part of ever since he had become a medic.

He turned back around and found Amber waiting for him. Taking his hand, she led him to her waiting car to drive to the graveyard.

The graveside service was little more than a shortened version of the funeral. The pastor once again exhorted the assembled to give their lives to God, for they knew not the day or the hour of their own passing. The clouds had been thickening since for over an hour, and as the pastor finished his sermon, the first drops of rain began to fall on the canvas pavilion erected over the small grave.

People began to leave, taking flowers from atop the coffin as remembrances of the day. Samantha chose a rose, and Robbie took a few daisies.

Soon, everyone was gone except Byron and Amber. With a firm but gentle voice, he told her to wait in the car. After she had gone, he reached out and snagged a tiny violet from a wreath. He placed it in his pocket and then simply stood there. The men tasked with the actual burial hovered about uncertainly, until one of them asked him if they could go ahead and begin the burial. Byron told them that that was fine. Then men began dumping shovels of dirt over the coffin, occasionally giving apprehensive looks over their shoulder at Byron.

Once they were completely finished, they walked to their work truck, and over the rising wind and rain, Byron heard one of them tell the other, "That dude gives me a major case of the heebie-jeebies, man. I mean, I felt fucking weird with him staring at us like that." The other man told him to shut his damn mouth and get into the truck.

Your buddy is right, boy, Byron thought at the retreating truck. *Give me a chance, and I may fill you with 5.56 NATO Green Tip and then forget all about it. I've done it before.* There was no real malice in the thought. It was just a simple declaration of fact in Byron's mind. Had he been holding his rifle, he might very well have shot the man for making that statement. *I need to get myself together.* He began to walk toward the car in the worsening rain. He was almost to the car when he caught sight of something at the peripheral of his vision. He turned his head and stopped dead. Standing in a row beside his daughter's grave were little girls. Three of them, all alike.

Get himself together? Who was kidding who here?

Too late, a voice whispered in the deepest parts of him mind.

Much too late.

Chapter Thirty-Two

The next few days were a blur to Byron. He woke, ate, slept a little, and then repeated the whole process. Dimly, he was aware that Amber was growing more and more concerned about him. Her questions were becoming more probing, and she no longer seemed satisfied with his vague answers. She mentioned Dr. Franklin more than once, and asked him continually if he was taking his medication. He told her that he most certainly was.

He had flushed every bit of medication he possessed down the toilet when had returned from Liza's funeral.

Byron knew that what was about to happen would cause Amber pain, and this distressed him greatly. However, this was how it had to be. Nothing less than this would work.

And he had to hurry, hurry. Time was running out. That damned clock was back, and running as fast as ever. This couldn't wait for long.

On the fourth day after Liza's death, Byron went into town and met with a lawyer. He made several arrangements and signed various papers. After he completed this task, he drove across town to a storage site, where all his parent's belongings, as well of much of his own, were stored. He had purchased the storage unit after his father had finally succumbed to lung cancer after a brutal struggle. Patricia had died a year before that, also of cancer. Hers was breast cancer that had spread so fast that she was dead only four months after learning she was ill. *Cancer seems to like my family,* he thought as he pulled into the site. *Maybe taking up smoking wouldn't have been such a hot idea.* He laughed at the absurdity of the thought.

He opened the unit and stood looking at the flotsam and jetsam of his early life and that of his parent's. He supposed he could have just given these things away, or sold them like he had his parent's home, but he couldn't bring himself to do it. It seemed to be too much of a defilement of their memory.

After standing there for a very long time, just looking back and forth over the cluttered boxes, he seemed to wake and moved into the unit. He began moving boxes from one side of the unit to the other, looking for a particular one. The storage rental place had insured against mice, but judging from the droppings, that assurance was a false one.

He had almost given up hope that the box he was looking for was even in the unit when he noticed that he had been standing with one foot on it for several minutes. He grunted something that might have been a laugh, or a sob. He sat down on the limited floor space and opened the flaps of the box. He looked at the contents for a while, and then stood. With a grunt, he hefted the box into his arms and carried it to his truck. He placed the box on the passenger seat and went back to close and lock the unit's door.

He drove to the Walmart in town and made several purchases. These made, he went back out into the damp heat of the day.

He drove back across town to the lake that butted up against the far side of the county. There were a few people milling about down around the shoreline. These people didn't bother Byron in the slightest.

The clock in his head was much more important.

Driving his truck down a rarely used lane that ran parallel to the lake, he parked under a thick canopy of leaves. He stepped out of the truck and just stood there for a bit, breathing in the mixed smells of pine and the lake. Then he turned walked over to the passenger side of the truck. He took the box to the back of the truck, where he lowered the truck's tailgate and put the box upon it.

He slowly unpacked everything from the box, laying each thing out in neat order. This done, he returned to the cab of the truck and brought out his purchases from Walmart. The fishing poles were pre-assembled, but he needed to attach hooks and sinkers to each. Once he had threaded the last hook into place, he stepped back from the truck and began to undress.

Once he was nude, he began picking up the articles he had lain on the tailgate and putting them on. The uniform was encased in plastic, and had not become too wrinkled. His medals shone brightly, with only a little tarnish on a few spots. These he fastidiously buffed back to a high luster. He slowly completed this task, and then went back to the front of the truck. Using his window as a mirror, he adjusted his beret to the correct angle. Stepping back, he gave his reflection a snappy salute. He right-faced and strode to the fishing equipment and collected it neatly under one arm. He made one more stop at his truck, getting into the glove box, and then closed the door and turned toward the lake.

With military precision, he walked down the small path that led down to the lake, a path he had trod so many times in his life, when it seemed that he had spent his entire summer vacations down here. He stopped at the small rock outcropping and stood looking out at the peaceful lake. He cast his mind back to the times Robbie and Samantha had accompanied him here, all those stingers of fish. He remembered the time that he and Amber had, on a dare, gone skinny dipping here. That little trick had come *very* close to ending their platonic friendship. He remembered the way the water had slid down her body, glistening in the moonlight. How had he managed not giving in to his entirely heartfelt desire to lay her down on that rock and make love to her that night? A missed chance, and one that he would never regain.

For once, he seemed to have the lake to himself, the super-charged fishing boats and jet skis absent. That was good. He didn't require an audience today. This was something he needed some privacy for, and was thankful that he was getting it.

He bent and proceeded to bait the hooks of the three fishing poles. He cast each one, and sat them side by side upon the rock. He wiped the dirt from the wriggling night crawlers that had gotten on his hands onto his handkerchief, and returned it to his pocket. He then stepped back and waited.

The clock spun backwards, nearing its terminus.

He stood at attention, his back ram-rod straight and staring straight ahead for over an hour. The clock reached zero with an audible click in his mind. The numbers flashed red.

At that instant, the middle fishing pole, the one that would have been Liza's, gave a jerk and began to screech as line played off the reel. With a spastic twitch, the pole shot off the outcrop and splashed into the lake. Byron could see it disappearing into the depths, a flash of brightness slicing through the dark water until it was no longer visible.

"See, baby girl? I told you. Fishies bigger'n Daddy."

Byron Williamson reached down and picked up the 9 mm pistol he had retrieved from his glove box. He placed it to his right temple, smiled, and pulled the trigger.

<u>Chapter Thirty-Three</u>

Amber awoke to the telephone, the ringing bringing her out of the deepest sleep she had taken since before Liza's funeral. Groggily, she looked at the clock on the bedside table and saw that it was still early afternoon. She felt a flash of aggravation. Everyone that knew her knew that she worked the 7-to-7 shift at Sacred, and that she normally wouldn't be awake for at least another hour. Everyone that knew her also knew that she had just endured one of the hardest weeks of her life, and would have had sense enough to let her sleep.

Therefore, it must be either someone that didn't know her, or someone that knew her and didn't give a damn. Either way, whoever had decided to wake her up was about to get a very illuminating lesson on why one doesn't wake up a nurse before she's ready to be awakened. She fumbled the phone from its cradle and held it to her ear.

"Yes?"

For a second there was no one there, and then Amber could hear the various noises in the background of the emergency room, a sound she could identify instantly. She listened to a woman's voice talking to someone at the desk, and then transfer the phone back. "Amber?"

"Yeah, it's me. Melissa?" Melissa Fry was another nurse at Sacred Heart E.R.

"Amber, hon, I hate to wake you up like this, but I think you need to come down to the E.R." There was a pause, and then Melissa said "Honey, there isn't any good way to tell you this. Byron's here. He's shot. It's a head wound, and it doesn't look too good."

Amber felt the breath leave her body. She could hear Melissa's voice, tinny and indistinct, as she lowered the phone back onto the cradle. With her arms wrapped around her knees, Amber Jennson began weeping.

She remained that way for several minutes, and then got up and began to find herself some clothing. She felt no inherent need to hurry. She was struck by a deep sense of deja-vu as she dressed. Hadn't she watched Byron dress in just this same fashion less than a week ago? And going to the exact same place? And, of course, for the exact same reason. Amber suffered no illusions about Byron's chances. She knew what to expect when she walked into that emergency room. She was going to say good bye to a man that she loved. She was going to have to prepare herself for that.

And she had just less than four miles to get ready for it.

Chapter Thirty-Four

It was dark. It wasn't cold, or hot for that matter, but it was certainly dark. He tried to get his bearings, to look about himself, but there seemed to be no up or down. He felt weightless, floating in all that darkness. He wasn't concerned yet, but he felt that he might get that way soon. There was a rhythmic wet noise, like water in a pipe. Well, there was that. He could hear, at least. The noise was almost like the surf at low tide, gently whispering up the sand and back out to sea. It was a comforting sound, in reality, and he was glad for it.

He tried to think, but it was difficult. Questions would almost form, and then slip away right before he was able to truly grasp them. He concentrated, and was finally rewarded with a complete and coherent thought.

Where am I?

As if that had primed the pump, fragments of thoughts began to bombard him. Colors, sounds, a kaleidoscope of sensory input, none of it connected. He began to feel a little frightened, but fought it. Panic was still at arm's length, but he was unsure of how long he could keep it there. He focused and tried to make sense of the chaos around him.

An image floated to the forefront of his mind, and he held onto it with all his will. He needed something tangible. The image was fuzzy at first, like looking through someone else's prescription glasses. Slowly, it began to sharpen. Water, calm water, bounded by rocky cliffs and pine trees. The image began to expand his senses, and now he could smell the pine. With an almost audible thud, he was suddenly standing on a rocky outcrop overlooking a lake.

He knew this lake, didn't he? It was all so familiar. He looked about himself and let the familiar sights sink in. Yes, he was sure of it, he knew this stretch of water. This was his lake, his fishing hole. It had been his favorite spot to fish when he was a child.

Had been his favorite spot to fish?

Why was he using the past tense? Why did he *feel* like the past tense, for that matter?

Okay, boys... hold the phone here.

Something was definitively *not* tracking. He looked back out onto the lake, and felt a bit calmer. There were some disturbing questions coming up here, and he wasn't sure he was ready to deal with any of that just yet. No, let's just stare at this lake. There's no hurry, so hold the phone, let's just chill for a bit.

He had no idea how long he stood there, looking out at the calm waters. Time didn't seem to be a very important thing here in this place. Wherever this place *was*. He could just go on looking at this lake for as long as he wanted. He didn't know how he knew that, but he did. About a million years of this sounded just about right to him.

He could feel other thoughts hovering around the fringes of his consciousness, but kept them at bay. They might be unpleasant, and it seemed to him that he had dealt with quite a bit of unpleasantness at some point. Far away, so low it was barely discernable was a sound he recognized. *Sikorsky UH-60 Blackhawk multi-role military helicopter*, his mind reported. The thought and the sound caused panic to well up inside him. With a mental scream, he shoved the thought back. Instantly, the low drone of the helicopter disappeared, and he was left with nothing but the soothing sounds of the forest and the lapping waters of the lake. Standing here with the breeze caressing him and looking at a lake that the sun never seemed to set on was all he needed right now.

After a few minutes (*days, years, millennia*), he sat down and crossed his legs. He noticed that he was wearing a very nice uniform, and he was momentarily *(eternally)* worried he might get the pants dirty on the bare rock, but then he shrugged and let it go. Letting things go seemed to be what this place was all about. Just look at the ease with which he had removed that annoying (and terrifying) helicopter. He glanced around and noticed that there was a fishing rod and a full can of bait lying next to him. With a sunny grin, he baited it and cast it out into the lake.

He played with the line a while (*forever, not at all*), and then decided that nothing would be grander than to just lie back and look at the passing clouds with his arms behind his head. So that is what he did. He watched the clouds chase one another across a perfect, robin's egg blue sky while he looked for shapes in them, as he had as a child. He was still doing this when he noticed that he wasn't alone.

He looked to his right, and his world collapsed in upon itself. Standing a few feet from him were three little girls, their coffee and cream colored skin glowing in the sun. Everything came back to him in a torrent. He knew everything, and he knew it instantly. He struggled to his feet, weeping, his hands held out to ward off this terror.

But from the children came three identical smiles of such beauty that he found himself weeping even harder, just from the joy of seeing it. He dropped to his knees in front of them and began trying to explain, telling them over and over how sorry he was, how so very sorry he was.

As one, the girls shook their heads. They walked toward him. He braced himself. They were here to give him his punishment, and he would face it gladly if he could finally set this stone in his heart aside.

As they came within touching distance of him, he closed his eyes and prepared for the pain he knew was soon to come. He was so steeled for horror that it took him several seconds to realize that the girls were kissing his tears away, running their hands through his hair. His eyes sprang open in amazement. They stood all around him, and their laughter pealed away into the perfect sky. Each girl came around to face him. They took his face in their hands and, one by one, kissed him on the soft flesh between his eyebrows.

When they spoke he could understand their language perfectly, even though he had not spoken Arabic since his time in Iraq, a lifetime ago. A peace unlike anything he had ever known filled his whole being. There was nothing to forgive, they told him. They felt nothing but love for him. And suddenly, he realized he felt nothing but love in return. These were his girls. *His.* He had paid for their sudden, unfair demise ever since that horrid April day in Iraq, and now he knew beyond any doubt that they were, in fact, okay. Dear God, so much more than okay. They had been ripped from the world by a madman with a weapon of pain and destruction, but now they were beyond the reach of any such men, now and forever. These were Byron's girls, and they were safe. They were happy.

They were perfect.

The oldest smiled at him and said in halting English, "Come, Byron ibn William, there are many fish to catch here, yes?"

He rose to his feet, laughing, tears of joy still falling like a gentle summer rain. They pulled at his hands and led him back to the rock outcrop. He was utterly unsurprised to find that there were now four fishing poles. With laughter, they set about casting them into the waters below.

Byron spent hours (*forever, infinity*) baiting the girls' hooks and helping them cast out into the placid lake. There was never so much as a nibble, but that suited Byron right down to the ground. If they never caught another fish, he would be perfectly content to sit here and fish with his girls.

This thought brought up another one of those disquieting bubbles of anxiety at the edge of his consciousness. Wasn't there something missing here? He had his girls, he had his fishing pole, the day was perfect… so why did he suddenly feel like there was something vitally important missing from this equation?

As he sat among the children, pondering this new thought process, he noticed another pole had appeared. He looked at it for a long moment. He suddenly remembered precisely when he had seen that pole last. It had been the last thing he had seen in his life, as a matter of fact.

The last thing he had seen in his life? What did that mean?

He became completely motionless when a very small hand came to rest on his shoulder. With the utmost care, he slowly turned his head. He slowly rose to his knees and turned. Standing with the sun backlighting her in a diffuse golden nimbus was Liza. The disease was banished from her, leaving only the beauty of his daughter in its wake. He opened his arms to her, and with a laugh of pure joy, she stepped into her Daddy's bear-like embrace. The girls all laughed and clapped their hands.

Behind them, the surface of the lake burst, and a fish jumped several feet out of the water and fell back with a colossal splash, its iridescent scales reflecting a million rainbows across the beatific faces of Byron and Liza.

And yes, it was much, much bigger than Daddy.

Chapter Thirty-Five

Amber walked towards the bay where Byron Williamson's body was being kept alive by machines. Her feet kept trying to veer off course, to the nurse's desk, to medical supply, to Egypt, anywhere but to that cold, sterile, curtained room that contained the man she had known and loved. She kept placing them one in front of the other mechanically, forcing herself towards that hateful place.

When she finally arrived at the bay, she stopped for a moment, taking several deep breaths and trying to mentally prepare herself for what she was going to see. No stranger to gunshot wounds, she knew the damage they could do, especially when they were to the face. Often, at close range, the escaping gases from the round caused more damage than the bullet itself. Depending on where the wound was located, Byron's face might look more like a Pokémon doll than his old self.

With a trembling hand, she slowly reached up and pulled the curtain back. Everything seemed to slow down. The whisper of the curtain across the tile floor sounded like the slow hiss of steam escaping a teapot just before it began to give off its signature wail. The light had been muted, dimly throwing a circle onto the bed. Byron lay perfectly still, the only movement the metronome-like rise and fall of his chest as the respirator kept his lungs full of air. His face was barely visible through the heavy bandages that wrapped his head, but his eyes were both visible. They twitched occasionally under his eyelids, but Amber knew better than to hope that meant anything. People with massive brain damage could move arms and legs at times. Melissa Fry appeared at her side, and slid her arm around Amber's waist. When she spoke, her voice was low-pitched with emotion.

"Amber, honey, he was an organ donor. They'll be prepping him in a few minutes, but I thought you would want a few minutes alone with him first."

Amber nodded, her eyes never leaving Byron's bruised and bloodied face.

After several moments of oppressive silence, Amber spoke. "Have Samantha and Robbie seen him?" she asked.

Melissa looked pained. "I called Samantha right after I called you. She just said that we needed to do whatever was necessary with his body. I asked her about bringing Robbie to say good bye and she told me that her son had seen enough dead people this week, thank you very much. Then the… well, the *bitch* hung up on me. Can you believe that? I mean, Jesus, he was Robbie's father, and…"

Amber cut her off with a slight shake of her head. "Lissa, Samantha is going to do what she thinks right. I may not agree with her, but it's her right to decide. And, to tell the truth, Robbie *has* seen enough members of his family die this week. Now, sweetheart, you've been the best friend I could hope for calling me like you did, but could you give me a few minutes before the organ harvest team gets in here?"

Melissa nodded and gave Amber a tight hug. "I'll be at the desk if you need me. I'll keep the harvest team occupied as long as you need me to."

"Thank you, Lissa."

Melissa left the room, and Amber walked to the head of the gurney. She took Byron's hand in hers, amazed at the life that still remained in it. He was brain dead, and without the life support equipment, he would be as inanimate as the bed he lay on. She looked at his closed eyes, purple and swelled from the force of the bullet that had ended his life. She closed her own eyes and tried to remember the last time she had seen those blue eyes, the spark of life dancing within them.

She had gotten the entire story from the attending physician, which thank God hadn't been Rutherford. If it had been, Amber was sure her tenure as a nurse here at Sacred would have come to an end. If she had seen that self-important little bastard gloating over Byron's body, she probably would have done her dead-level best to blind him for life.

The gunshot had been heard by a game warden that was in the area following up on a tip that there were some men hunting whitetail deer out of season. The warden had gone to investigate and found Byron lying face-down on the rock that they had spent so much time fishing from when they were kids, blood spreading in an ever-widening pool around his head, his beret somehow still clinging to his head.

The warden had thought Byron dead where he lay, until he noticed the labored respirations coming from his chest. Grabbing his radio and calling in for EMS, the warden had done what he could to stem the bleeding from Byron's head with his dark brown uniform jacket. It broke Amber's heart to see the pain in the man's eyes as he held his blood-soaked jacket bunched up in his hands, the bright brass Game Warden badge standing out in stark contrast to the dun-colored material, looking at it as if it wasn't real.

EMS had arrived within a few moments, and found a pulse. They worked on Byron all the way to Sacred, giving it everything they had to give because this was one of their own, and they weren't about to lose him, but the attending physician, a young doctor named Paulus, had seen that there was nothing that could be done for Byron, and had called the code. With a sad sigh, he called the time of death for the record and walked out of the room, shaking his head. The EMS crew that had worked Byron were alternating between weeping and using some of the vilest language on earth when Amber arrived at Sacred. They met her at the door, but words failed them. They settled for giving her a hug and a gentle kiss on the cheek.

Paulus was working on Byron's chart when Amber arrived. He apologized to Amber for being unable to revive Byron several times, beginning to jabber before she had laid a hand on his cheek and told him that it was all right, she knew he had done his best.

The warden had described the scene, Byron in his Class A uniform, and the fishing poles. Amber had listened for as long as she was able, and then turned to the bay where Byron lay.

She had felt almost every emotion a human being is capable of on the ride over to Sacred. When she arrived the last of the red rage had just burned its way out of her heart, leaving a small, smoldering coal deep inside. Now, she felt a deep, almost eerie calm. She doubted that feeling would last, but she was glad for it. She thought it might stand her in good stead right now to be able to keep her cool over the course of the next few hours.

Standing by his side, she looked at the pile of his clothing discarded in the chair. In the rush to save his life, his uniform had been cut away. It laid on the chair now, the top of the olive green stiff and maroon with Byron's blood. His row of decorations had managed to remain clear of the blood splatter, and Amber reached over and, very carefully, removed it and his name tag. She also very gently reached around the gauze wrapped around his head until her fingertips felt the metal chain on his neck. Working it around, she found the release and slip Byron's dog tags off. She refastened the chain and wrapped them around the medals. Reaching into a drawer, she removed a Number 10 scalpel and set about meticulously cutting Byron's patches off his uniform. She took all of these things and placed them gently into one of the patient belonging's bags she found in another drawer, and then padded them with several pillowcases.

Robbie might not feel anything but hatred and sorrow towards his father right now, but one day he might want something of his dad's, and Amber thought that these small mementos might suffice. At any rate, it was better than nothing at all, which is most certainly what Samantha had of Byron's to give to Robbie.

She had passed her eyes studiously over the decorations, something she had heard Byron laughingly call his "salad bar" in happier times, as she was sure she would do again and again in the coming months. She had no idea what the multi-colored ribbons and medals meant, but was sure she would find out soon. That's what the internet was for, right?

She raised her eyes back to Byron. She stared at him intently, following every curve and hollow that was visible under the gauze with her eyes, understanding now about that clock he had described, seeing it perfectly in her mind, those numbers rapidly rolling away to nothing.

She leaned down and planted a gentle kiss on his pliant, still-warm lips.

"I love you, Byron. Know that, please. Know that I love you."

She reluctantly laid his hand back on his chest and was turning to leave when something caught her eye. She turned back, and her breath caught. For a moment, she thought she might simply pass out from oxygen deprivation. With a strangled gasp, she started breathing again. She looked at what had caught her eye.

She stared for a long, long time.

On legs that felt numb, Amber slowly re-crossed the room. She stopped in front of the chair that held Byron's uniform. Sitting atop it was Liza's favorite stuffed bear. It had not been there seconds before. She knew that beyond a shadow of a doubt. Had she not just picked up that uniform to remove those decorations? There had been nothing there, certainly not something as noticeable as a little girl's teddy bear. That was the sort of thing that would have been hard to miss, especially since the last time she saw it, that bear had been in Liza's coffin with the lid being closed over it. The bear should be in the arms of a beautiful little girl, now buried under six feet of earth.

But it wasn't. It was here, sitting on her Daddy's uniform.

Amber picked it up and held it to her cheek. She could smell the mingled scents of both Byron's rough bearded face and Liza's sweet baby-soft hair. While those smells seemed like they should have been incongruous, but they complimented each other perfectly, the musk of Byron and the smell of Liza's baby-soft skin creating the most perfect scent Amber had ever encountered in her life. Two tears slid slowly down both sides of her face. She closed her eyes and breathed in the love from the teddy bear. Yes, that's what the scent was, love. Amber had never thought that an emotion could have a physical scent, but now she knew exactly what love smelled like.

When she opened them again, her eyes were clear and a calm, beautiful smile infused her face with a soft glow.

"Thank you, Liza-Bug. Tell your Daddy that Amber loves you both. I'll see you again someday. Don't catch all the fish without me."

Amber Jennson walked out of Sacred Heart Regional Hospital and into the falling dusk of the Tennessee summer, that smile of singular beauty still shining from her face.

The End

Ryan S. Pack was born and raised in Eastern Kentucky. He lives there still with his wife LuAnn and their four children. He was an Emergency Medical Technician for fifteen years before an injury ended that career. He has since spent his time in and out of college, where he remains one credit shy of a degree, and writing what he refers to as "My Ramblings". This is his second edition of Fishing With Liza.

© 2014

Everything contained herein is a work of fiction. All the characters are part of the author's imagination. No part of this work may be used without the express permission of the author.

www.ingramcontent.com/pod-product-compliance
Lightning Source LLC
Chambersburg PA
CBHW071134170626
46809CB00002B/615